VOLUME III

by **Debbie Dadey**
and
Marcia Thornton Jones

illustrated by **John Steven Gurney**

SCHOLASTIC INC.

New York Toronto London Auckland Sydney
Mexico City New Delhi Hong Kong Buenos Aires

Witches Don't Do Backflips, ISBN 0-590-48112-6, Text copyright © 1994 by Marcia Thornton Jones and Debra S. Dadey. Illustrations copyright © 1994 by Scholastic Inc. Book design by Laurie Williams.

Skeletons Don't Play Tubas, ISBN 0-590-48113-4, Text copyright © 1994 by Marcia Thornton Jones and Debbie S. Dadey. Illustrations copyright © 1994 by Scholastic Inc. Book design by Laurie Williams.

Cupid Doesn't Flip Hamburgers, ISBN 0-590-48114-2, Text copyright © 1995 by Debbie S. Dadey and Marcia Thornton Jones. Illustrations copyright © 1995 by Scholastic Inc. Book design by Laurie Williams.

Gremlins Don't Chew Bubble Gum, ISBN 0-590-48115-0, Text copyright © 1995 by Marcia Thornton Jones and Debra S. Dadey. Illustrations copyright © 1995 by Scholastic Inc. Book design by Laurie Williams.

12 11 10 9 8 7 6 5 4 3 2 1   5 6 7 8 9 / 0

Printed in the U.S.A.   40

This edition created exclusively for Barnes & Noble, Inc.

2005 Barnes & Noble Books

ISBN 0-7607-9541-X

First compilation printing, May 2005

Contents

Witches Don't Do Backflips

To Rebekah Dadey and Collin Baker —
may your lives be full of magic!

With thanks to Amanda and Kevin Gibson for
technical advice — DD and MTJ

1

Pink Tights and Tutus

"There's no way I'm going to wear funny-looking black tights," Eddie told Liza, Melody, and Howie. The kids were on their way to Brewbaker's Gym. Brewbaker's was a new gym and many third-graders from Bailey Elementary School had signed up for gymnastics classes there. First the four friends had stopped off at Eddie's aunt's house to feed her dog, Prince Diamond. Eddie promised to feed and to take care of her full-blooded Dalmatian while she was on vacation in Las Vegas.

When Eddie lifted the latch to slip out of the backyard, Diamond darted out. Eddie lunged after him, but all he caught was a mouth full of dried leaves as he fell on his face.

1

Melody giggled. "You look like you could use a few gymnastics lessons!"

Eddie spit out a twig and glared at her. "You can forget about any sissy lessons until we catch Diamond. Aunt Mathilda will cook us for dinner if anything happens to her new dog!"

Eddie and his friends chased after Prince Diamond, but the big spotted dog was too fast for them. He zigzagged around the front yard until the four friends were out of breath from chasing him.

"We'll be late for our first class if we don't catch him soon," Liza whined.

Howie shrugged. "I think he just wants some company. Why don't you let him come with us?"

Melody nodded. "Maybe he'll learn something besides scratching fleas."

"All right," Eddie agreed, "but it would be fine with me if we missed a silly tumbling class." As the four kids walked away from Aunt Mathilda's house, Prince Diamond trotted along beside them.

Melody laughed as she hurried along. "I think Eddie would look great in a pink tutu."

"That's it!" Eddie turned to walk away. "You won't catch me wearing any frilly ballerina stuff. I'm not going."

Howie grabbed his friend's arm. "This isn't ballet. It's gymnastics. And you're not going anywhere. If I have to do this, then so do you. Now, come on or we'll be late."

"Why does your mother want you to take lessons, anyway?" Eddie asked and continued walking with his friends.

Howie shrugged and watched a robin sitting on a fence post. "She said it'll help me be more graceful."

"Graceful!" Eddie yelled. "Boys don't need to be graceful!"

"My dad said football players take

dance and gym classes," Liza said. "It helps them to be more flexible."

"They probably wear pink tights and tutus," Melody giggled.

Eddie reached for Melody's pigtails. "I'll show you what I think of tutus."

"Quiet." Howie pointed to the gym at the end of Forest Lane. "There's somebody out front."

The four kids looked at the new building. It was two stories of solid black glass; even the door was black. In front was a porch of black marble with big black columns. Sweeping the porch was a short-haired figure dressed in black tights, black sneakers, and a black baseball cap.

"It's the teacher," Liza whispered. "Her name is Miss Brewbaker. I met her when Mom signed me up for the class."

"I've never seen so much black in my life. Hasn't she ever heard of colors?" Melody asked.

"It's depressing if you ask me," Howie said.

"Gymnastics lessons are depressing," Eddie complained.

"Don't be such a worrywart," Melody said. "I bet it'll be fun."

"Just like the black plague," Eddie mumbled. The woman on the porch stopped her sweeping, pulled the black baseball cap firmly down on her head, and waved at the kids.

Liza, Melody, and Howie waved back, but Eddie giggled. "Take a look at the size of her nose. If she sneezes, we'll end up somewhere over the rainbow. Look, she even has a wart on that huge honker."

"Eddie," Liza said softly. "That's not a wart. It's a mole. Besides, she can't help the size of her nose."

"Just like you can't help having red hair and freckles and being rude," Melody told Eddie.

Eddie held up his hands. "Don't get

your pigtails tied in a knot. I wasn't making fun of her. I was just stating facts."

"The fact is she's a nice lady who's going to show us how to do flips and cartwheels," Liza said.

"We'd better go inside and get this over with," Howie muttered.

"Don't worry," Liza told him. "It'll be good exercise."

Eddie shook his head. "Yeah, I wonder what kind of torture that 'nice lady' has in store for us."

2

Flying

Miss Brewbaker smiled and propped her broom against a shining black column as the kids walked up the yellow brick sidewalk.

"Somebody should have taught her to floss," Eddie snickered softly. "Then she wouldn't have lost that tooth."

Melody elbowed Eddie in the side and whispered, "She's not missing a tooth. That's just a big space in front. Lots of people have them."

"Like the space you have between your ears?" Eddie muttered.

Melody stuck her tongue out at him and then smiled at Miss Brewbaker. "We're here for gymnastics."

"Of course," Miss Brewbaker said in a deep voice. "Follow me." She turned and disappeared inside the black door. The four kids looked at each other. Howie shrugged and climbed the stairs.

"I hope she's a better teacher than she is a dresser," Eddie said.

"My mom says Miss Brewbaker is a top-notch gymnast from Europe." The four kids looked behind them at Carey, a girl from their class. Carey skipped up the steps, her blond hair bouncy and full of curls.

"What happened to your hair?" Howie asked.

"It looks like she fell in a bucket of hair curlers," Eddie joked.

Carey patted her curls. "I got a perma-nent." She smiled and turned around so everyone could see the back of her head.

"Miss Brewbaker may be a good gym-nast," Melody said, ignoring Carey and pointing to the doorway, "but she's a terrible house cleaner. She could at least knock down these spiderwebs."

"We'll do it for her," Liza suggested, reaching for the broom.

"NO!" Miss Brewbaker shouted as she appeared in the doorway.

"We don't want to waste valuable tumbling time. Please, come in." Then she pointed a long fingernail at Prince Diamond. "But make sure that horrible, mangy mutt stays outside."

Diamond whined and lay down under a tall tree. Overhead, a squirrel skipped along a branch and chattered. When the squirrel hopped on to a telephone wire and scrambled around the building, Diamond dashed after him.

"That ought to keep Diamond busy during our class," Eddie said as the kids followed the gym teacher inside.

Miss Brewbaker led them past a steep staircase and down a dark hallway. Their footsteps echoed on the black-and-white tile floor.

"For a new building it's awfully dark," Liza said softly.

Miss Brewbaker peered down at her and smiled, showing the large gap between her teeth. "Sorry about that we haven't finished putting in all the lighting in the halls yet." Then she led them into a large room. It was completely empty, except for black mats covering the floor.

"Ick!" Liza called out. She pointed to a big, black spider crawling across the floor.

Miss Brewbaker smiled. "Do not be frightened of the spider. She is quite harmless."

"I hope this class is harmless," Howie blurted.

"We don't think we'll like gymnastics," Eddie told Miss Brewbaker.

Miss Brewbaker looked at Eddie and pulled her baseball cap firmly down on her head. Then she pushed a button on a tape recorder. The strong beat of a rock song made the windows rattle. Miss Brewbaker put her hands on her hips and yelled, "Watch what you can learn! You may even get to perform at the festival this month." Every year Bailey Elementary had a Halloween festival.

Miss Brewbaker clapped her hands and winked. Then she ran and did three cartwheels in a row without using her hands. Her body swirled through the air like a giant black cloud.

"Wow! That lady can move!" Howie whistled.

Carey nodded. "I told you she was good."

When Miss Brewbaker reached the end of the mat she did three backflips, jumping so high it was as if she hung in mid-air.

"Look at her soar!" Melody squealed.

Eddie stared at Miss Brewbaker and slowly nodded his head, "You're right, it DOES look like she's flying."

3

Rhyme Time

Miss Brewbaker did another backflip and landed right beside the five kids. Melody and Liza clapped their hands and Howie nodded. But Carey put her hands on her hips and shook her head. "I can't do that," she wailed. "It'll mess up my new hairdo!"

"You have such pretty golden locks," Miss Brewbaker purred. She reached out

and touched one stray curl. Then she winked and spoke deeply in a singsong voice:

> *"Straight or curly*
> *Black or gold*
> *You'll love tumbling*
> *When all is told!"*

Carey stood off to the side, watching the other kids try their luck at somersaults and cartwheels. She laughed every time Liza tried to do a cartwheel.

"Quit laughing at her," Melody warned. "You're not doing any better."

Carey shook her head so her curls swirled around her face. "I could, but I don't want to mess up my hair."

"If anything was going to mess that mop up, it would be the way you keep slinging it around," Melody told her. "You're just using your hair as an excuse."

"Am not!" Carey snapped.

"Then prove it," Eddie dared.

"Okay, I will!" Carey went to the end of the mat and took a deep breath. She took a tiny hop and skip before sending her feet sailing in a perfect cartwheel.

"Lovely!" Miss Brewbaker clapped from a corner of the room. "You are a very talented gymnast."

Carey smiled. "I'll bet that I can get even better with practice!" Then she cartwheeled across the room so fast, her legs looked like the spokes of a wheel.

"Wow," Liza sighed, "it's just like Miss Brewbaker said."

"That's right," Eddie said slowly. "Her rhyme came true."

Howie grinned. "If only she'd help Liza do a cartwheel, too."

Carey walked across the mat like the winner of a gold medal in the Olympics. "Liza always ends up sitting down hard on her rear."

"Be quiet," Melody snapped. "You'll hurt her feelings."

"But it's so funny," Carey giggled. She was right. Liza just couldn't get her legs straight up. Instead, they always swung sideways, throwing her off balance. By the end of the lesson, Liza was in tears.

"I'll never be able to do it," Liza sniffed.

Miss Brewbaker glided over the mats. She wiped a tear from Liza's cheek and patted her on the back. Then she spoke in her deep singsong voice:

> *"Replace that frown,*
> *No time to cry!*
> *Keep on practicing and*
> *Soon you'll fly!"*

Liza looked up at Miss Brewbaker. "Do you really think I can?"

"I know so!" Miss Brewbaker said firmly. "Now try once more."

Liza looked at her friends and sniffed

before running down toward the mat.

Howie clapped and Melody did a little cheer as Liza finished a perfect cartwheel. "Yeah! You did just as well as Carey!"

Liza grinned and clapped her hands. "It's so easy all of a sudden."

Eddie didn't say a word. The other four kids said good-bye to Miss Brewbaker and then all five gymnasts walked onto the porch. The black glass door slammed shut behind them.

"Isn't he adorable?" Liza pointed to a fat cat perched on the porch. The cat stopped licking his paws to blink his huge amber eyes at the kids.

Eddie took one look at the cat and said, "My grandmother says black cats are bad luck."

"I think he's cute," Liza said and petted the cat until he closed his eyes and purred.

"That's Merlin, my cat," Miss Brewbaker told them as she stepped on to the porch with her broom.

"Merlin, what a ridiculous name for a cat," Eddie said after they were on the sidewalk, away from Miss Brewbaker.

"Merlin was the wizard in the King Arthur stories," Howie said. "My dad read them to me. Merlin was pretty neat."

"I like that name," Liza said. "It's magical."

Eddie looked back at the tall black building, the black cat, and the high flying gymnastics teacher sweeping the porch. "Magical is just the right word," he said softly.

4

Witch's Broom

Eddie slurped the last of his chocolate milk and looked at his friends. "Don't you think Miss Brewbaker is odd? Normal people don't talk in rhymes." Eddie, Liza, Melody, and Howie sat at the kitchen table at Melody's house, having a snack.

"I think she's neat," Liza said, munching on a chocolate chip cookie.

"You just like her because she showed you how to do a cartwheel," Melody said.

"That *was* strange," Howie said. "Right after Miss Brewbaker said that rhyme, Liza did a perfect cartwheel."

"The same thing happened with Carey," Eddie pointed out.

Liza slowly sipped her milk. "That's

because Miss Brewbaker is a good teacher."

Eddie threw his napkin into the trash can. "If you ask me, there's something spooky going on at that gym."

"I wasn't going to say anything, but I noticed something, too," Howie said. "When we went inside, Miss Brewbaker left her broom on the porch."

"So?" Melody said. "My mom does that all the time."

"But when we went outside, the broom wasn't there. Miss Brewbaker carried it with her when she came outside." Howie wiped his mouth with a paper napkin and looked at his friends.

"A broom can't move itself," Melody said.

"Not unless it's a magical broom," Eddie told them.

Melody giggled. "I think Eddie's in la-la land."

Eddie ignored Melody. "Think about it.

It all adds up: a moving broom, strange rhymes that come true, and flips that look like flying."

"It adds up to what?" Liza asked.

Eddie slapped the table. "Don't you guys get it? Miss Brewbaker's a witch."

Liza and Melody broke into a fit of giggles. "That cold milk froze Eddie's brain," Melody snickered.

"Miss Brewbaker is not a witch," Liza blurted.

Melody nodded. "Liza's right. Witches don't teach gymnastics."

"And they definitely don't do backflips," Liza added. "Haven't you ever read any fairy tales? Witches fly through the air on brooms."

"Exactly," Eddie interrupted. "Just like Miss Brewbaker's broom. If she's a witch, it would explain how the broom moved."

"You have to admit," Howie told the girls, "it was pretty creepy the way Carey and Liza were able to do cartwheels after

Miss Brewbaker chanted those rhymes."

Melody stood up from the table. "I can't believe you could be so silly. You're just saying this because she has a big nose and a wart."

"A mole," Liza reminded her.

"Whatever," Melody said. "People can't help the way they look."

"Melody's right. You're being mean. I think you're just trying to get out of taking gymnastics. Miss Brewbaker's great and I'm not afraid of her. As a matter of fact, I'm going back there right now," Liza said.

"Why?" Howie asked. "The next class isn't until tomorrow."

Liza shrugged. "I forgot my gym bag and it has my house key in it."

Melody looked out the window. It was already starting to get dark. "Why don't you stay here? You can call your mom at work."

"No." Liza shook her head. "I've already

lost one house key. Mom was mad because we had to change all the locks. You're not afraid of Miss Brewbaker, are you?"

Melody shook her head. "I'm not afraid."

Eddie shook his head and muttered, "I'm not afraid, but I'm not going back there."

"Yes, you are," Melody said and

grabbed Eddie by the arm. "Be right back," Melody yelled to her mom.

The four kids walked out of Melody's house and back toward Brewbaker's Gym with Prince Diamond trotting behind them. Several dogs barked at them as they strode through the neighborhood.

The building was totally dark as the kids walked up the yellow brick sidewalk. A flock of crows flew overhead. "This

place is creepy in the evening," Howie gulped.

"It doesn't look like anyone's here," Melody said.

"Liza, why'd you have to leave your bag?" Eddie complained.

"Yeah," Howie said, "I'd rather be home scrubbing trash cans than going inside here."

"It'll just take a second," Liza said as she walked up the shiny black steps. But before she could knock on the door, a small black creature slid across the porch and twisted itself around her legs.

"Aaahh!" Liza screamed. "It's got me!"

5

Frog Legs and Spider Stew

Liza jumped and knocked into Miss Brewbaker's broom, sending it crashing to the floor of the porch. The loud noise sent Diamond into a barking fit and the black animal at Liza's feet hissed. As soon as the dog noticed the cat, he flew up on the porch. Merlin arched his back, hissed, and quickly swatted the dog's wet nose before springing off the porch. Prince Diamond lunged after him and both animals raced around the building.

"It was just Miss Brewbaker's black cat," Melody said with relief. "There's no reason to be scared."

"I wouldn't be so sure," Eddie said. "A black cat is bad luck, especially when it's a witch's cat."

"You've got a hairball stuck in your

brain," Liza said. "I'm not afraid of a black cat. I was just startled, that's all."

Melody slapped Eddie on the back. "Your imagination is getting the best of you. There are no such things as witches or ghosts or goblins. And I'll prove it to you."

"How?" Howie asked.

"Easy. Liza's forgot her gym bag, right?"

Liza, Eddie, and Howie nodded.

"It's obvious that no one is here, so all we have to do is walk in and get Liza's bag. While we're at it, we'll take a quick look around. I'm willing to bet all my Halloween candy that we won't find anything but smelly old gym socks."

"We can't just walk in there," Liza told Melody. "That's snooping."

"We have to get your key, don't we?" Melody asked as she slowly pulled on the door. "Oh, no, it's locked," she said. "We'll have to go around back."

"What if someone sees us?" Howie warned. "They might call the police."

Melody shrugged. "We'll just tell the truth. We're looking for Liza's gym bag."

Melody stepped over Miss Brewbaker's broom and hopped down the shiny steps, leading her friends to the back of the gym. Long shadows covered the lawn and a chilly October breeze moaned through the tree branches. Somewhere in the distance they heard Prince Diamond howling. Melody tried the back door. Slowly, it opened. Inside, the building was pitch-black.

"Follow me," Melody whispered and went inside. "I think the gym is this way." The four kids walked down the wide empty hallway.

"I smell food," Howie said.

"There's supposed to be a health food snack bar here," Liza said.

"What if Miss Brewbaker is cooking frog legs and spider stew for a snack?"

Eddie said sarcastically as they waited for Melody to open a door.

"Hope you're hungry," Liza giggled.

The door slowly swung open, letting a sliver of light escape into the hall. "Oh, my gosh," Melody said, stepping back.

Her three friends pushed around her, gasping at what they saw.

"This proves it," Howie whispered.

6

Hansel and Gretel

The four kids stood in the middle of a small kitchen, staring at the biggest gingerbread house they'd ever seen. Its roof was covered with bright gumdrops and the sides were smothered with peppermint icing. Strawberry licorice outlined windows of lemon drops and the sidewalk was made out of jelly beans.

"That's a fabulous gingerbread house," Liza whispered. "It covers the whole table. I bet it took Miss Brewbaker days to make it."

Eddie nodded and reached out to pluck a gumdrop from the roof.

"Don't touch that!" Howie hissed.

"Why not?" Eddie asked. His hand was frozen over the colorful roof. "No one will miss one measly gumdrop."

"That's exactly what Hansel and Gretel thought," Howie told him. "And they almost ended up as witch pudding."

Liza shook her head. "Miss Brewbaker is not a witch but you shouldn't mess up her house. That took a lot of work to build."

"Come on," Melody said, "let's get your bag. The gym must be behind the other door." Melody turned to go out of the kitchen but then she stopped suddenly. "Wasn't Miss Brewbaker's broom on the porch?" she asked.

Liza nodded. "I knocked it over. We'll have to set it back up before we leave."

"We won't have to," Melody said with a tremble in her voice. "Because it's already been picked up and put away."

"What are you talking about?" Howie asked.

Melody pointed to the hall. There,

propped beside the door, was Miss Brew-baker's broom.

"How did it get there?" Liza asked.

"It flew," Eddie said seriously.

"Brooms don't fly on their own," Liza told him.

"You're right," Eddie whispered. "They usually come with a witch." Before his friends had a chance to say anything, a shrill cackling came from deep within the dark building.

"What's that?" Liza whimpered.

"I think Eddie's witch just flew in!" Melody said. "Let's get out of here."

"But I can't leave without my key," Liza cried.

"Come on!" Eddie called over his shoulder as he raced down the dark hall and out the back door.

"You'll stay with me, won't you?" Liza asked Melody.

Just then another haunting laugh sent goose bumps racing down their backs.

Melody's eyes got big and she slid around the broom, keeping her back to the wall. When another high-pitched screech echoed throughout the building, Eddie pushed Melody all the way out the back door.

Liza heard the back door shut, then she slowly headed for the only other door in the hallway.

7

Bubbling Brew

The building was deathly still as Liza crept down the long, dark hallway. "There's no such thing as witches. There's no such thing as witches," Liza whispered to herself. She didn't really believe Miss Brewbaker was a witch, but a moving broom and dark hallways were enough to scare her.

Finally, she reached the door and held her breath while she opened it. It was the gym, filled with black gym mats.

Outside, the brisk autumn wind rattled the tall tree's branches, making them scrape against the black window. Liza spied her gym bag nestled in the corner, and tiptoed across the soft mats. Just as she reached out to grab the handle, the room was flooded with light.

"Why, hello my little pretty," Miss Brewbaker said softly.

Liza jumped around and stared at Miss Brewbaker standing in the doorway, her arms loaded down with groceries. "I . . . I left my bag," Liza stammered. "My house key is inside."

Miss Brewbaker nodded. "I'm surprised you were able to get in. I thought I locked the door."

Liza looked down at the smudge on her sneaker. "We figured you already went home, so we tried the back door," she explained. "It wasn't locked. We saw your gingerbread house, too."

"I see." Miss Brewbaker smiled. "It will be a lovely donation for the Fall Festival, don't you agree?"

"The festival?" Liza whispered. "You made that beautiful house for the festival?"

"Of course," Miss Brewbaker told her. "What else would it be for?"

Liza started to tell her that witches used gingerbread houses to lure and trick kids, but instead she snapped her mouth shut. She didn't want to hurt Miss Brewbaker's feelings.

"Get your key and come with me," Miss Brewbaker told her. "You may help me with these groceries. I bought a few treats for my students."

Liza carried a bag of groceries into the small kitchen and watched while Miss Brewbaker took out a big black pot from a cabinet. "I thought I would have a warm drink before going home," she told Liza.

"Hot chocolate is my favorite," Liza said.

"This is not exactly hot chocolate," Miss Brewbaker said. "It is an ancient recipe passed down by my family. A secret recipe." Miss Brewbaker opened another cabinet and pulled out the oldest book Liza had ever seen. The cover was made from bumpy black leather and the pages were yellowed with age.

When Miss Brewbaker gently opened the book, dust floated like a cloud above the pages. She used a pointy black fingernail to follow the list of ingredients. Then she gathered six bottles from a shelf. They were filled with strange yellow and purple spices. Miss Brewbaker carefully sprinkled a pinch from each jar into the kettle, added some water, and stirred the mixture with a big wooden spoon.

When the mixture bubbled loudly, Miss Brewbaker took out two tall black mugs with pictures of cats on them and poured the brew into the mugs. To Liza, the mixture looked like thick pea soup.

"Would you like to join me?" Miss Brewbaker asked, holding the mug out so Liza could smell the spicy aroma.

Liza stared at the bubbling brew and

shook her head. "N . . . no thank you. I have to go home. Thanks for letting me get my gym bag, and it was nice of you to make that gingerbread house for the Fall Festival."

Miss Brewbaker shrugged. "It is only something I whipped up. Besides, Halloween is my favorite holiday."

Liza picked up her gym bag and took one last look at the beautiful gingerbread house before walking down the hall. "Good-bye, Miss Brewbaker," Liza yelled as she pulled open the back door.

When the door opened, Merlin darted in with Prince Diamond close behind.

"Diamond, get out of here!" Liza cried, racing after the big spotted dog. Both animals ran straight into the kitchen where Merlin jumped on the counter behind Miss Brewbaker. Diamond skidded to a stop and cocked his head. Before Liza could reach him, Diamond jumped up and licked Miss Brewbaker right across the nose. Miss Brewbaker wiped her face and pointed a skinny finger at Diamond before saying in a singsong voice:

"Leave us be,
We don't like dogs.
Especially spotted ones
Like warty frogs!"

Then Miss Brewbaker sneezed so hard, Prince Diamond dropped back down to the floor. His toenails clicked on the tile as he smelled around the kitchen. Prince Diamond whined once and then put his front paws on the table.

"Get that creature before he eats the gingerbread house!" Miss Brewbaker screamed. Then she sniffed, pointed at

Prince Diamond, and said in her singsong voice:

> *"Hop away, hop away,*
> *You big bag of fleas.*
> *Get out of my kitchen*
> *And stay away. Please!"*

"He doesn't mean any harm," Liza explained as she grabbed Prince Diamond's collar. "I'm sorry. I'll make sure he never gets in here again." Then Liza dragged Prince Diamond out the back door.

Liza kept her hand hooked in Prince Diamond's collar as she headed away from the gym. She was halfway down Forest Lane when Howie, Eddie, and Melody jumped out from behind a bush.

"We were just coming back for you," Melody explained. "We didn't mean to leave you there all by yourself."

Liza glared at her friends. "You did too. You're a big bunch of chickens!"

"We are not!" Eddie snapped.

"Then why did you run?"

Howie shrugged. "You could have come too."

Liza held up her bag. "I had to get my key and you know it. You should have helped me."

"At least we sent Prince Diamond in after you," Eddie defended himself.

"You did not," Liza told him. "He was chasing Merlin and he really made Miss Brewbaker mad."

Melody nodded. "I guess we panicked. We're sorry, aren't we?" Melody looked at Howie and Eddie, but they weren't listening anymore. They were too busy staring at Prince Diamond.

"Something is wrong," Howie said softly. "Something is very wrong!"

8

Frog City USA

Prince Diamond was whining and turning around in circles. Then he sniffed and took three steps back toward Brewbaker's Gym.

"Get back here," Eddie said sternly. Prince Diamond looked at Eddie and whined. Then, before anyone could stop him, the huge dog dashed down the street and disappeared into the shadows of the night.

"Diamond!" they all screamed at once. "Come back!"

But the night was quiet except for the wind blowing scattered leaves. "I have to get him, or Aunt Mathilda will have a fit."

"But it's already dark," Melody said. "We have to get home."

"Melody's right," Liza agreed. "We'll never find him now. We'll help you look for him first thing in the morning."

Howie nodded. "Diamond will probably go home on his own as soon as he gets hungry."

Eddie looked nervously down the street, hoping to catch a glimpse of Diamond. "Are you sure he'll be all right?"

"Positive," Howie said.

The next morning was Saturday. Liza,

Howie, Melody, and Eddie were up early, searching the neighborhood for Prince Diamond. They were worried about Aunt Mathilda's dog. The more they yelled for him, the more concerned they became.

"Diamond has never stayed away so long," Eddie told his friends. "He likes being a nuisance too much."

"Sort of like you," Melody kidded.

"This is no time for jokes," Eddie said. For once, he was totally serious. "Diamond is a good dog," he said. "I hope nothing's happened to him."

Liza patted Eddie on the back. "Don't worry. We'll find him."

"Maybe he's chasing Merlin again," Melody suggested.

Liza shook her head. "He'd better not. Miss Brewbaker would have a fit."

Howie rubbed his chin. "Liza, did Miss Brewbaker see Diamond last night after gym?"

"See him?" Liza said. "Why, Diamond practically kissed her on the lips."

"Oh, no!" Howie said. "It's worse than I thought."

"It's all right," Melody said. "No one ever died from kissing a dog. Kissing Eddie, maybe, but not a dog."

Howie ignored Melody and grabbed Liza's shoulders. "This is important, Liza. Did Miss Brewbaker say a rhyme about Diamond?"

"How did you know?" Liza asked. "She said two of them about frogs and dogs."

Eddie slapped his forehead. "Miss Brewbaker's done something to Diamond. My Aunt Mathilda is never going to believe this."

"Don't be silly," Liza told them. "Miss Brewbaker is *not* a witch and she didn't do anything to Diamond. That silly dog is probably sleeping in your Aunt Mathilda's backyard."

"I'll go check," Eddie said hopefully.

While Eddie jogged down the street, his three friends continued looking in nearby yards. They hadn't looked long when a scream sent them racing after Eddie.

Eddie stood in the middle of Aunt Mathilda's backyard. He pointed to the bottom of a weeping willow tree and screamed again as Howie, Melody, and Liza skidded to a stop in the grass.

"What's wrong?" Melody gasped.

Eddie turned to look at his friends. His face was as gray as the clouds in the sky. "We have to stop that tumbling mad woman!"

"What are you talking about?" Liza asked.

"I'm talking about what she did to Diamond!"

Howie, Melody, and Liza glanced around the yard. "I don't see anything," Howie said.

"Look closer," Eddie told them, pointing to a little green frog with big black spots.

Melody's eyes got big and Howie sucked in his breath.

"You don't really think that's Prince Diamond," Liza said.

Eddie crossed his arms and nodded like he'd just won a presidential debate. "I told you that Miss Brewbaker spelled trouble."

Melody kneeled down to pet the frog's bumpy skin. "You can't prove this is Diamond. For all we know, it's just a freckled frog."

"What if it is Diamond?" Howie asked. "We have to find out for sure."

"How?" Melody asked. "If she is a witch, she might turn us all into frogs!"

"There's only one thing to do," Howie said seriously. "We have to find out how to stop her. And I know where to find all the information we need."

Without another word, the four kids marched toward the Bailey City library with a little frog hopping close behind.

9

Operation Research

Dark storm clouds rolled over Bailey City and a cold wind sent leaves whirling. Rain splattered the windows of the library as Liza, Eddie, and Melody waited for Howie to find what he needed. He searched up and down several shelves until he spotted a fat green book. He carried it to the checkout desk and waited. Mr. Cooper was too busy talking to another librarian to notice them.

"It's got me in a dither," Mr. Cooper sighed. "I'm just lost without my little Snookems. The house is like a graveyard without her padding around the house after me, and I just can't sleep unless I hear Snookems's cute little bark."

The other librarian nodded. "Old Mrs. Farley says the same thing about her poodle. I can't imagine where those two dogs have wandered off to, but I'm sure both of them will turn up soon."

"Where could they be?" Mr. Cooper said with a hopeless sigh. "I've looked everywhere, but all I can find are nasty frogs."

Eddie gasped, and Howie nearly choked. "Did you say frogs?" Melody asked.

Mr. Cooper nodded at the children standing by the checkout desk. "I've never seen so many frogs before in my life. I guess that rainy spell we had last winter had something to do with it."

"It's a spell, all right," Eddie muttered.

"What did you say?" Mr. Cooper asked.

Howie shoved the big book he was holding at Mr. Cooper before Eddie could say anything else. As soon as Mr. Cooper saw the book, he shook his head. "You're always checking out this book. Maybe you should try reading something else,

like a good mystery. I'd be happy to show you some."

Howie smiled politely and shrugged. "It's a fat book. It takes a long time to read."

"Hummph," Mr. Cooper mumbled as he checked out the book and returned Howie's library card.

"Thank you," Howie said, grabbing the book and heading toward a table with his friends. "I hope you find your little dog!"

The four friends sat in a corner of the library. All around them, kids were reading fun holiday stories, but Liza, Howie, Melody, and Eddie didn't notice. They stared at Howie as he opened the big book to the index.

"What are you looking for?" Melody whispered.

"Proof," Howie answered. "I think Eddie's right about Miss Brewbaker being a witch, and I plan to figure out what we can do to get Diamond back."

Liza put her hands on her hips. "Miss Brewbaker didn't do anything to Diamond. He's probaby off chasing squirrels somewhere."

"Then explain the spotted frog being right where Prince Diamond likes to stretch out," Eddie dared her.

"Easy," she said. "It's just like Mr. Cooper said. The rainy weather brought tons of frogs to Bailey City."

"But what about Snookems and the poodle?" Howie asked.

Melody nodded. "I bet Miss Brewbaker zapped them into tiny little frogs."

Liza giggled. "Miss Brewbaker wouldn't do that. She's too nice."

Howie slowly shook his head. "I wish you were right, Liza. But I'm afraid Miss Brewbaker can't stand dogs. Remember she called Diamond a mangy mutt?"

"So?" Liza said. "I don't like hamsters, but that's not a crime!"

"It *is* a crime if you change dogs into frogs!" Eddie yelled.

"Shhh!" Mr. Cooper warned. "You children will have to hop along if you can't be quiet!"

"I wish he hadn't said hop!" Melody muttered.

Howie sighed. "I think those rhymes that Miss Brewbaker keeps saying are really witch spells."

Liza rolled her eyes. "That's not true! Miss Brewbaker is nice. After all, she showed me how to do a cartwheel."

Melody shrugged. "Cartwheels today and flying on broomsticks tomorrow."

Howie tapped the fat book in front of him. "I have a plan." The four kids huddled together as Howie shared what was in the book. "There are two ways to stop a witch's spell," he began.

"You're as batty as a witch's attic,"

63

Melody said as soon as Howie was finished.

Eddie stood up from the library table. "We have no choice. We have to help Prince Diamond . . . before it's too late."

10

Witch's Cookbook

The cold, drizzling rain continued as the four friends hurried to Brewbaker's Gym. A cool wind rattled the brightly colored leaves of the trees overhead.

Liza shook her head when they stopped in front of the black building. "I still don't think Miss Brewbaker is a witch. But I did notice something strange when I was in the kitchen."

"You mean besides the fact that she had a gingerbread house big enough to feed half of Bailey City?" Eddie asked.

Liza nodded. "Miss Brewbaker has a very unusual cookbook. She used it to make her brew. It's very old and too fancy to be an ordinary cookbook."

"Maybe it's a witch's cookbook!" Melody said.

"And it has recipes for spells!" Eddie agreed.

"Great!" Howie slapped his hands together. "Now that we know where the spell book is, I know just what to do. We'll keep Miss Brewbaker busy with gymnastics while one of us sneaks into the kitchen."

"Just be careful," Melody warned.

"Be careful about what?" Carey asked from behind them, causing all four kids to jump.

"We were talking about how dangerous gymnastics can be," Melody fibbed.

Carey flung her curls around her head and opened Miss Brewbaker's gate. "I'm so good, I don't have to worry about it. You're the ones who should be careful."

"I'd like to carefully rearrange your face," Eddie muttered before Howie pulled him onto the yellow brick sidewalk.

"Come on," Howie said. "We've got to help Diamond."

The black building's shiny windows stared down like evil eyes as the five children climbed the steps and pushed open the door. "Are you sure we should do this?" Melody asked.

Howie opened his mouth to answer, but he didn't have a chance. Just then Miss Brewbaker appeared with a big smile. She wore the same black baseball cap pulled down over her short hair, and she held a huge basket filled with shiny red apples. "Good morning, children. How about a snack before we get started?"

"Thanks," Eddie said and reached out to take the biggest apple.

Howie grabbed Eddie's arm, yanking it back. "We'd better not. We wouldn't want to get sick when we're turning flips."

Miss Brewbaker shrugged and went over to the mats. Liza and Carey ran over and started showing Miss Brewbaker their cartwheels.

Eddie frowned at Howie. "What's the big idea?" Eddie complained. "I was hungry."

"Did you just crawl out from under a rock?" Melody whispered. "Haven't you ever heard of *Snow White and the Seven Dwarfs*?"

"Yeah, and you're being just like that dwarf Dopey," Eddie giggled.

"You're the dope," Melody said under her breath. "The witch in that story puts Snow White to sleep by giving her a poison apple."

"Don't worry about me." Eddie smiled.

"I'm too tough for poison." He walked over to Miss Brewbaker and picked up the basket of apples.

"I'd be happy to take these to the snack bar for you," Eddie said sweetly. Eddie carried the basket past the kids. He licked his lips as he headed down the hall.

"You don't think Eddie would be stupid enough to eat one of those, do you?" Melody asked Howie softly.

Howie shook his head. "If he does, it will be the last thing he chomps down on. He'll be dreaming until a princess kisses him. And that would be forever!"

11

The End of Rhyme

"Come on over, children. I want to show you a new flip," Miss Brewbaker called to the class. "We have an exhibition tomorrow and this flip will impress your parents. It will be great practice for those of you chosen to perform at the Fall Festival."

The four kids concentrated on the flip Miss Brewbaker was showing them. She flung her legs up and did five flips in a row to the end of the mats and then did five more flips back to the kids.

"That's a round-off," Carey informed them. "I'm sure I can do it."

Miss Brewbaker smiled. "I'm sure everyone will be able to do it by the end of the lesson."

Howie shrugged his shoulders and

tried. He ended up in a lump on the floor. "This is dangerous," Howie complained. "I could have broken my neck!"

"You're right," Miss Brewbaker said. "Gymnastics can be very dangerous."

"Especially when your teacher is a witch," Melody mumbled to Liza. Liza shook her head and rolled her eyes.

Miss Brewbaker helped Howie up. "It is important to never try dangerous flips without a mat and an instructor. That is why I am here." Then Miss Brewbaker patted Howie on the head and chanted:

> *"Through the air*
> *You will fly,*
> *Never afraid*
> *Of soaring . . . "*

"High!" Howie hollered.

"Oh," Miss Brewbaker said, in surprise, "so you like to rhyme, do you?"

Howie nodded. "I've taken it up recently. So have my friends."

Melody, Liza, and Carey looked at each other. "We have?" Liza asked.

"How about this one?" Miss Brewbaker pulled her black baseball cap down firmly on her head and chanted:

> *"Up and down*
> *My broom will go*
> *With all the children*
> *Lined up in a . . . "*

"Row!" Howie shouted.

Miss Brewbaker stomped her foot, adjusted her hat, and did three backflips. Her body swirled through the air like a black fog.

"What are you doing?" Melody asked. "You're making her mad."

"The library book said that finishing a rhyme takes away the spell's power," Howie reminded her.

Miss Brewbaker did three backflips and turned up the visor of her cap. "How about this one," she said.

> *"Four little kiddies*
> *Too cute to stop*
> *Now is the time*
> *For you to . . . "*

"Hop!" Liza shouted and clapped her hands.

Miss Brewbaker looked at her and

jumped up and down. Then she bounced around the room faster and faster.

"I think Miss Brewbaker has flipped out," Carey said.

Melody ignored Carey and looked at Liza. "If you didn't believe she was a witch, why were you so quick at finishing that rhyme?"

Liza shrugged. "I said that just in case. I don't want to be a frog."

"Here we go again," Howie interrupted as Miss Brewbaker headed toward the

kids. "I hope you girls are good with rhymes."

Miss Brewbaker stopped her flipping and panted:

> *"Topsy-turvy,*
>   *End over end*
>   *You and I*
>   *Were meant . . . "*

Howie, Melody, Liza, and Carey looked at each other.

"What's a word that rhymes with end?" Howie shouted.

Carey, Liza, and Melody shrugged their shoulders. Then suddenly Liza smiled and yelled, "Were meant to be friends!"

Miss Brewbaker pulled off her cap but instead of flipping, she smiled at Liza.

Liza smiled back at her and said:

"We have won
This game of rhyme
As friends we'll have
A much better time!"

Miss Brewbaker put her cap back on and started laughing. She pointed her finger at Liza and said:

"I give up
You have me beat
But I like you kid,
I think you're neat!"

"Do you really mean it?" Liza giggled.

Miss Brewbaker nodded. "Of course, I do. You are a wonderful tumbler and have a great ear for rhyme. I'd be proud to have you as my friend."

"What about Prince Diamond?" Howie asked.

Miss Brewbaker looked confused. "Who is Prince Diamond?"

Melody stepped forward. "Diamond is the big spotted dog that you turned into a frog!"

Miss Brewbaker's smile faded and she pulled her cap off. "Dogs don't interest me, especially ones that chase Merlin. Now, you must run along. Don't be late for tomorrow's exhibition."

The four kids grabbed their bags and ran out of the building. They didn't stop until they were at the end of the yellow brick sidewalk.

"Oh, no!" Howie yelled. "We forgot about Eddie. He's still in there! What if Miss Brewbaker finds him snooping in the kitchen?" The four kids looked back at the house. From inside they heard an eerie cackling. Then all was silent.

"What if Miss Brewbaker turned him into a frog?" Melody said.

Carey laughed. "What are you talking

about? Eddie isn't a frog, even though he might be a little slimy sometimes!"

"Very funny, bunny brains," Eddie said from behind them.

"Eddie, you're all right!" Melody threw her arms around him and gave him a big hug.

"Let go of me," Eddie snapped. He pushed her away and took a big bite from a huge red apple. "Of course, I'm all right. I *told* you I was too tough for a witch."

"What happened?" Howie asked.

Eddie spoke softly. "I found the cookbook, or rhyme book, or spell book, or whatever you want to call it. Then I said each one backwards, just like Howie said in his plan. I bet it broke every one of Miss Brewbaker's spells."

"I think you're right," Melody laughed as Prince Diamond came loping up and licked her right on the nose.

"Diamond!" Eddie yelled and hugged the big dog around the neck. "I'm so glad to see you!" Just then Merlin darted out from under a bush. Diamond gave a quick yelp, and raced down the street after the black cat.

"No!" Liza screamed. But she was too late.

12

Sleeping Beauty

"Where's Eddie?" Liza whispered the next day.

"He's going to miss the whole thing if he doesn't get here soon," Melody said softly. Miss Brewbaker's students were waiting to perform their flips for their parents.

Howie looked at his parents in the audience and waved. Next to Howie's mom sat Mr. Cooper with Snookems. "Maybe Prince Diamond ran away again," Howie said.

"I thought we'd never find him yesterday," Liza said.

"That dog is going to drive us crazy," Melody muttered. "He's always running off."

"Speaking of driving us crazy," Carey said. "There's Eddie now." The four kids watched as Eddie's grandmother dragged him through the door of the gym. Eddie yawned and walked over to line up with the other gymnasts.

"He looks like Sleeping Beauty," Liza giggled.

Carey shook her head. "There's nothing beautiful about Eddie." The kids had to agree that Eddie had never looked worse. His hair was mussed, his ball cap was on sideways, and he had dark circles under his eyes. He yawned again on his way over to them and nearly tripped on his untied shoelace.

"Oh, no!" Melody suddenly remembered. "Eddie ate that apple yesterday. Maybe Miss Brewbaker really did have a magic spell on it! He looks like he can't wake up."

"I didn't eat a rotten apple," Eddie

snapped. "I let Prince Diamond sleep in my room so he wouldn't run away again. He kept me up half the night, licking me in the face!"

"You mean he kissed you?" Howie asked.

Eddie rolled his eyes. "I wouldn't exactly call dog slobber a kiss."

Melody jumped up and down. "Diamond saved your life! If he hadn't kissed you last night you'd be in dreamland after eating Miss Brewbaker's magic apple."

"That's right." Howie nodded. "A kiss from a prince is the only thing that can save you from a witch's poison apple. Prince Diamond saved you."

"What's all this stuff about magic and witches?" Carey asked.

Liza shook her head. "These guys think Miss Brewbaker is a witch and her rhymes are magic spells."

Carey rolled her eyes. "That's the craziest thing I've ever heard," she said, looking at the yawning Eddie. "After all, witches don't do backflips."

Skeletons Don't Play Tubas

To Marcia from Debbie
To Debbie from Marcia
— from one old bag of bones to another

1

Bailey City Cemetery

"Boo!" Eddie jumped out from behind a big tree and waved his baseball cap.

"Eddie!" Liza screamed, grabbing her friend Melody. "You scared me to death!"

"I told you it was a mean thing to do," Howie said, coming from behind the same tree.

"You guys are as jumpy as cats on Halloween," Eddie said, pulling his cap down over his curly red hair.

Melody shook her black braids. "You didn't scare me, but you have to admit this place *is* creepy."

It was early in the morning and the four friends were in the Bailey City Cemetery collecting leaves for a school project. Huge trees filled the cemetery and large red and yellow leaves littered the ground.

"But it is the best place to collect leaves," Howie said, holding up a handful of brightly colored leaves. "I bet I have ten different kinds already."

"Look at this one," Liza said, holding up an orange leaf. "It's really different."

"Talk about different, look over there." Eddie pointed. "That has to be the strangest-looking fellow I've ever seen."

The four kids looked at a very tall, very skinny man. He was holding a huge black box and walking toward them.

"I have never seen anyone so skinny," Melody said.

"Or so pale," Liza added. "He looks half dead."

"Maybe he is dead." Eddie snickered. "After all, we're in the cemetery."

Liza shivered. "His box is bigger than he is."

Eddie giggled again. "That's probably his coffin."

Just then the skinny man looked at the four kids and smiled, showing huge yellow teeth.

"Let's go!" Liza squealed and ran out of the cemetery. Her three friends followed her as fast as they could. The tall, skinny man was coming toward them.

2

Skeletons in the Closet

Eddie, Melody, Liza, and Howie raced all the way to Bailey Elementary School. They stopped under their favorite oak tree to rest.

"Why did you run?" Eddie asked Liza.

Melody agreed. "That man must think we're rude."

"I'd rather be really rude than really dead." Liza shuddered. "That guy gave me the creeps."

Howie nodded. "He is a stranger. We shouldn't talk to strangers."

"Especially ones that follow us!" Eddie said. He pointed to the stranger lugging his huge black box up the stairs of Bailey Elementary.

"Let's see what he's up to," Melody

suggested as the skinny man disappeared inside the school.

The four friends climbed the steps to Bailey Elementary. It was early in the morning, and no other students had arrived yet. They made their way silently down the hall until they could peek into the office. That's where they saw the tall skinny stranger talking to their principal, Mr. Davis. Principal Davis was a large, bald, egg-shaped man.

"If Principal Davis sat on that guy, he'd be chalk dust." Eddie laughed.

Melody smiled. "Mrs. Jeepers always needs more chalk. Maybe she could just use that fellow's bald head."

Eddie slapped Melody on the back. "If there were any more bald men around here we could start a baldy circus. We'd get rich selling tickets."

"It's not nice to make fun," Liza said as Principal Davis looked their way.

"Students, I'm glad you're here," he

said, pulling them toward the thin stranger. "I'd like you to meet the new band teacher, Mr. Belgrave. He is going to teach us how to play instruments."

Melody and Howie smiled at the new teacher, but Eddie looked at Principal Davis and said, "We've never had a band teacher before."

"Then it's about time!" Principal Davis slapped Mr. Belgrave on the shoulder. "Our new teacher is a real trouper. He is going to teach in the old science room, otherwise known as the storage closet."

"In the closet?" Liza asked.

Principal Davis nodded. "Since the school's so crowded, it was the only place to put the band class."

Mr. Belgrave smiled. His big yellow teeth stood out against his pale white skin. For the first time, the kids heard him speak. His voice came from deep inside his chest. "I look forward to seeing you in band class."

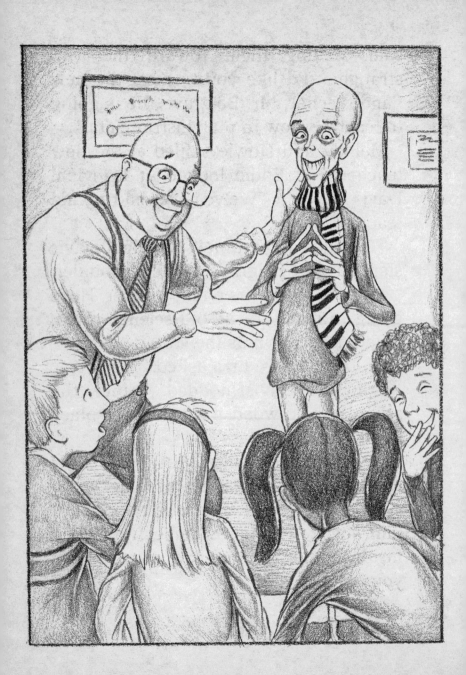

The four kids backed away and hurried down the hall toward their classroom. Eddie stopped before he went inside the room. "There's no way I'm going to learn music from that fellow. He looks like somebody sucked all the life out of him!"

"Maybe it was Mrs. Jeepers," Howie said, half-seriously. Many kids in their third-grade class thought that their teacher might be a vampire.

Melody shook her head. "Mr. Belgrave has probably been sick. He can't help it if he looks like death warmed over."

"I know he can't help it," Liza complained, "but he scares me. He looks just like a skeleton."

"Right," Eddie said seriously. "Just like a skeleton in a closet."

3
Moaning

"These are hard to make," Melody said. The whole third-grade class was making leaf print place mats to sell at the Fall Festival.

"It's stupid," Eddie said. "Adults are always thinking up hair-brained ideas to keep us busy."

"I wish we could make jack-o'-lanterns for Halloween instead of these things." Liza sighed.

"Shhh, Mrs. Jeepers might hear," Howie whispered, pointing to their teacher.

But Mrs. Jeepers did hear. She looked up from the papers she was grading and said in her Transylvanian accent, "I do not care to be associated with jack-o'-lanterns. They were originally used to ward off the dead. These place mats are much more cheerful." Mrs. Jeepers smiled her odd half smile and then went back to grading papers.

Howie nodded and held up a bright orange leaf. "We have to remember it's for a good cause, to make money for the school."

Eddie shrugged. "I just don't feel like making place mats."

Melody wiped paint off her fingers. "Nobody wants to make these, but we have to. So get busy!"

"I don't *have* to do anything!" Eddie smiled and tapped the pile of leaves on his desk. "Oooops!" he said as yellow leaves fluttered to the floor. "I'd better pick these up."

Eddie dropped to the floor and slowly began collecting his leaves. While he was crawling around, he tied the shoestrings of a girl named Carey to her chair and put Liza's book in Melody's desk.

Eddie was crumbling up a yellow leaf for Howie's notebook when the noise started. It started like a low hum. Then it grew louder and louder until the windows rattled.

"What is that?" Howie gulped. Liza's eyes got big and Melody's mouth dropped open.

"It sounds like a snoring elephant," Eddie said.

All the kids looked at Mrs. Jeepers in time to see her odd little half smile. "The new band teacher must be warming up his tuba," she said. "Which reminds me. It is time for us to have band class."

"Band class?" Eddie jumped up into his seat. "We have to go to band class?"

"Yes." Mrs. Jeepers smiled and rubbed the green brooch at her neck. "We are very fortunate that everyone may participate by playing an instrument. I am sure you will enjoy it. Now, line up."

"I'd rather eat wool coats," Eddie mumbled as he got up from his seat.

Mrs. Jeepers flashed her eyes at Eddie. "Did you say something?" she asked.

Eddie gulped and lied. "I said, I can't wait to play some notes."

The kids were quiet as their class walked down the hall to the new band room. Mrs. Jeepers watched as her class silently filed into the tiny room.

The room was crammed full of chairs and instruments. There were drums, violins, saxophones, flutes, trumpets, and a huge tuba that hung on the wall. Liza didn't notice the instruments, though. She was too busy staring at what was standing beside the tuba.

It was large. It was white. It was a skeleton!

4

Claude

"This is my good friend, Claude," Mr. Belgrave smiled, showing his big yellow teeth as he patted the skeleton on the head.

"Your friend?" Liza gulped and tried to scoot her chair away from Claude.

Mr. Belgrave nodded. "I couldn't find anyplace to put him, so I just left him here so he could enjoy the music."

"I don't think his ears work very well," Eddie teased.

Mr. Belgrave's teeth flashed another big smile. "Oh, you never know. Claude may be a real music lover. But enough about him, let's begin by passing out the instruments."

In just a few minutes, Mrs. Jeepers and Mr. Belgrave had helped almost everyone

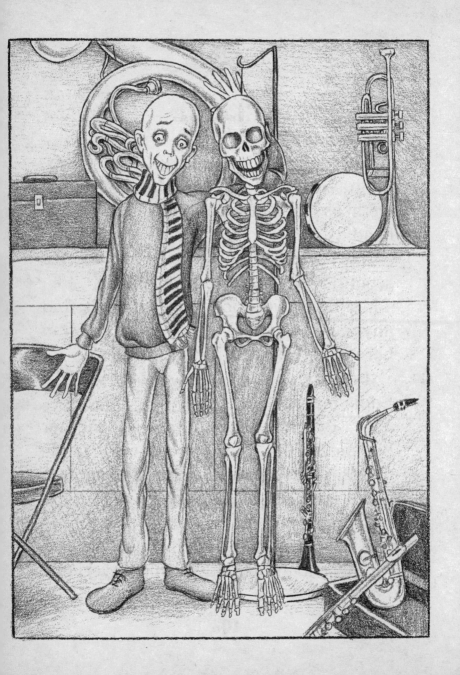

choose an instrument. Melody examined her flute as Liza tried out the valves on her saxophone. Howie tried to figure out how to hold his trombone, but Eddie had already figured out how to work the cymbals. *Cling! Cling!* Everyone's ears rang with the sound.

Cling! Cling! Eddie was having a great time clashing the cymbals together. *Cling! Cling!* Mr. Belgrave blinked twice and tapped his conductor's wand on a music stand, trying to get Eddie's attention. But Eddie couldn't hear him over the clanging cymbals. *Cling!*

When Mrs. Jeepers flashed her eyes in Eddie's direction, the rest of the class froze. Melody kicked his shin to get him to stop.

"What's the big idea?" Eddie asked. "I was just getting warmed up."

Mr. Belgrave smiled his big toothy grin and finished giving out the instruments. "No one wants the tuba?" he asked. "It's just as well. It's the only instrument I can't play."

"Really?" Mrs. Jeepers looked surprised. "I was certain I heard tuba music earlier."

Mr. Belgrave shook his bald head. "It wasn't me."

"Maybe it was Claude," Eddie piped up.

Mr. Belgrave smiled. "Maybe it was."

"Students," Mrs. Jeepers said, walking out the door. "I leave you in Mr. Belgrave's capable hands. I am sure you will give him your complete attention."

Mr. Belgrave smiled and picked up his conductor's wand. "Let's begin," he said in a low voice.

"But we don't know the first thing about these instruments," Melody said. "You can't seriously expect us to play."

Mr. Belgrave looked deep into her eyes. "I am dead serious," he told her and motioned for everyone to begin.

A squeaking, honking, banging sound

filled the air. By the end of the hour, Mr. Belgrave had given each student a few tips on playing their instrument, and the noise almost sounded like music.

"I felt like I was really playing in there." Howie smiled as they walked back to their classroom.

"I never knew music could be such fun," Melody agreed.

Eddie nodded. He'd had a great time banging the cymbals, but he noticed Liza hadn't said a word. "What's wrong?" he asked her. "Skeleton got your tongue?"

Howie gasped and Melody shrieked when they looked at their friend. Liza's skin was deathly pale.

5

Toe-tapping Tunes

Liza tugged Melody's arm, pulling her down a side hall. Eddie and Howie followed close behind. When they lost sight of the rest of the class, Liza gathered her three friends in a tight huddle.

"What's gotten into you?" Melody asked. "You act like you've seen a ghost."

"It wasn't exactly a ghost. But it sure was dead," Liza said, her eyes wide.

"What are you mumbling about?" Eddie snapped. "Either you saw a ghost or you didn't."

Liza took a shaky breath before explaining. "Do you remember that skeleton in the band room?"

Melody nodded. "Mr. Belgrave called it Claude. Isn't it cute that he named him?"

Liza squeezed Melody's arm tight. "Only if you call a living skeleton cute!"

"A living skeleton?" Melody, Eddie, and Howie said together.

"You're nuts," Howie told her. "Claude is a science display. He's probably made out of plastic."

"Then what made Claude's toes tap along to our music?" Liza asked.

Eddie pecked Liza's forehead with his finger. "I think your brain has been tapped."

Liza knocked Eddie's hand away and frowned. "Remember, I was sitting next to that stack of bones. While you were blowing hot air into your instruments, something caught my attention. At first, I thought it was all your blowing moving a piece of paper on the floor. But then I looked closer. That's when I saw it."

"What?" Melody asked.

"Claude's toes were tapping out the same rhythm we were playing," Liza said. "And I saw it with my own eyes!"

"Maybe you need glasses," Howie suggested.

Melody nodded. "The only tapping going on was Mr. Belgrave's wand when he was trying to get Eddie's attention."

"But I saw it!" Liza insisted. "That skeleton was listening to us. It was like our music made him come to life."

"Are you saying our music was bad enough to wake the dead?" Eddie joked.

"Maybe," Liza said seriously. "Or maybe he was already alive."

Melody patted Liza on the back and ignored Eddie's giggles. "Claude can't be alive," she told Liza. "His toes were just wiggling from the vibrations of all the musical instruments."

Howie nodded. "Melody's right. A little vibration and a lot of imagination. That's all there is to it."

Just then, a low tune echoed down the hall. Liza rubbed the goose bumps on her arms and looked at her friends. "Then who's playing the tuba?" she asked softly.

6

Music Lessons

"I'm not sitting by Claude again," Liza hissed. It was the next day, and the third-graders at Bailey Elementary were waiting to file into the new band room.

Eddie rolled his eyes. "Don't worry, I don't think Claude is going to flirt with you."

"Tease all you want," Liza told him. "But there's something strange about that skeleton."

"Okay, okay," Eddie said. "I'll sit next to Claude just to keep you from complaining."

Mr. Belgrave handed each student their instrument as they walked in the door. Melody took her flute and waited for Liza to get her saxophone. Eddie grabbed his cymbals and Howie took his gleaming trombone. Claude stood in the back of the room, just like yesterday. Liza peered up at his blank grin and shivered. But Eddie just grinned back.

"Howdy, Claude," Eddie said. Then he reached out and shook the skeleton's bony hand.

A funny look came over Eddie's face, and he quickly let go of Claude's hand. "That's weird," he said. "His hand feels warm."

"So?" Melody asked.

Eddie shrugged. "I figured it'd be cold. After all, he isn't alive."

Howie sat in the chair next to Eddie and slid the slide on his trombone. "The sun shining through the window probably warmed it up."

Eddie nodded. "Right. That must be it." Then he giggled and sat down with his back to Claude. "I'm beginning to sound like Liza!"

Liza scowled at him, but she didn't

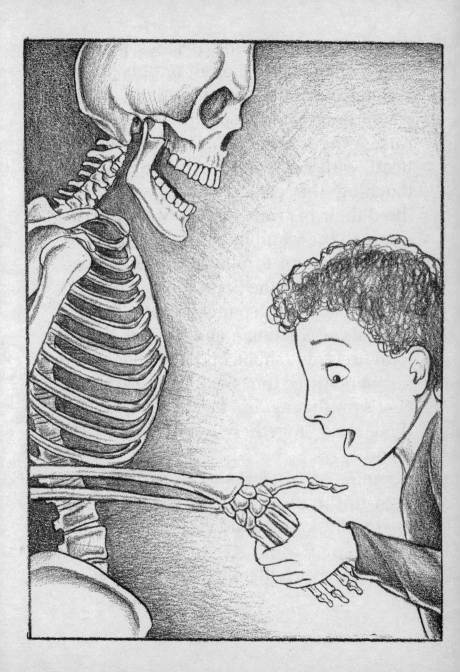

bother saying anything. Besides, Mr. Belgrave tapped his baton on his music stand, calling the class to order.

Mr. Belgrave stood up straight and raised the conductor's wand over his head, with his long skinny arms almost touching the ceiling. All the students lifted their instruments. As Mr. Belgrave dropped the wand in a graceful arch, the students began to play. Only the sound that came from the band room was nothing like music. It sounded more like fingernails scratching a chalkboard.

Mr. Belgrave shook his head and tapped his wand three times on the music stand. "Let's try that again," he suggested. "This time, stay together by watching my wand."

Again, Mr. Belgrave raised his wand high in the air and then let it fall. And again, the kids pounded, and blew, and tooted.

For nearly a half hour, the third-graders

worked on staying together and finding the right notes. But to Eddie, it sounded worse and worse. Of course, he wasn't having any trouble with his cymbals. He had already figured out the best way to bang the gleaming circles of brass together for the loudest crash.

While the rest of his friends were struggling with their instruments, Eddie looked around the old science room. Dusty beakers and test tubes lined the shelves and a broken film projector stood in the corner. A big silver tuba was squeezed in between Claude and the shelves. Eddie looked at Claude again. Something struck him as odd. Was it his imagination or had Claude's empty grin turned into a big frown?

Just then, Mr. Belgrave tapped his conducter's wand on the music stand and sighed. "No, no, no. You just don't seem to be getting it. Claude can play better than that. Let me show you."

The young musicians watched their new band teacher take long strides across the room and open a tall coat closet. He reached inside and pulled a shining trumpet from the shelf.

"You play the trumpet?" Carey, who was sitting in the front row, asked.

Mr. Belgrave smiled his yellow toothy smile and nodded. "Of course. This is my instrument of choice. I am especially moved by the sound of 'Taps' being played. Now, let me show you how to play 'The Bailey Elementary March.' "

Mr. Belgrave took a deep breath. His pale cheeks puffed as he blew and his fingers danced like spider legs on the valves of the trumpet. A smooth line of notes floated from the instrument, and even Eddie was impressed.

"Now watch again," Mr. Belgrave instructed them. "Notice how the notes

hang on to each other like they belong together."

With another deep breath, he played the melody as the children listened. It was a catchy tune, with notes that went high and then low like a roller coaster. Melody moved her head to the beat and Liza was swaying with the music.

"Quit tapping me," Eddie hissed to Howie. Eddie felt the drumming of his friend's fingers on his back. "You're giving me a headache."

But Howie was too busy watching Mr. Belgrave to pay any attention to Eddie. The annoying tapping continued.

Eddie elbowed his friend. "I said to stop!"

This time Howie looked at Eddie. "I'm not doing anything to you!" Then Howie went back to watching Mr. Belgrave.

Eddie sat very still. If it wasn't Howie

tapping him on the shoulder, who was it?
Eddie stiffly turned his head and looked
over his shoulder, right into the grinning
face of Claude.

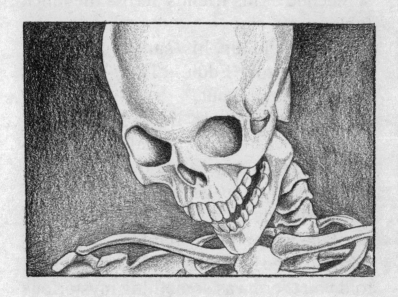

7

Dancing Skeletons

"I'm telling you Liza is right!" Eddie screeched at his friends across the lunch table.

Howie held up his sandwich. "Calm down," he told Eddie. "There's nothing to get excited about."

"Don't get excited?" Eddie squealed. "A skeleton was trying to dance with me and you tell me to calm down!"

"There's got to be a logical explanation," Melody said, wiping the milk off her face with a paper napkin.

Liza folded her arms across her chest. "I told you there was something mysterious about that skeleton, but you wouldn't listen."

Eddie rolled his eyes. "It kills me to say

this, but you were right. That skeleton is alive!"

Howie dropped his sandwich onto his lunch tray. "Hold on just a minute. Mr. Belgrave may be a little strange, and he definitely needs to find a good dentist to clean those yellow teeth. . . ."

"But he doesn't have living skeletons in his band room," Melody interrupted.

Eddie pointed his straw at Melody. "How can you be so sure? After all, remember where we first saw him?"

"In the cemetery," Liza whispered, her face pale.

"Exactly." Eddie nodded. "And it doesn't take a rocket scientist to know that there are skeletons in cemeteries. I'm telling you we've got to do something about Mr. Belgrave and Claude."

Howie gulped down another bite of his sandwich. "I think you're getting all excited over nothing."

"You won't think it's nothing when all

the skeletons in the Bailey City Cemetery come to life! Mr. Belgrave may even be planning on turning us into skeletons!" Eddie said seriously. "We need to stay away from him."

Howie and Melody both laughed but they stopped short when they heard a strange moaning sound.

"It's the tuba again," Liza said softly.

"It must be Mr. Belgrave," Melody said. "I bet he was lying about not being able to play the tuba."

Eddie shook his head and pointed across the room. "It's not Mr. Belgrave. He's over there." The four friends stared at their tall, skinny band teacher getting lettuce from the salad bar.

"I bet Claude is playing it," Liza said softly. "Remember Mr. Belgrave said Claude could play the song better than us."

Eddie, Melody, and Howie looked at Liza in surprise.

Melody rolled her eyes. "You're crazy," she said.

"It can't be Claude." Howie shook his head. "Skeletons don't play tubas."

"It is Claude," Eddie agreed firmly. "And I'm going to prove it!"

8

Special Guest

As soon as they got back to their classroom, Liza whispered to Eddie. "How are you going to prove that Claude is alive?"

Eddie shook his head. "I don't know yet, but I'll figure out something. You try to. . ."

"Shhh," Liza said. "Mrs. Jeepers is looking at us."

Their teacher, Mrs. Jeepers, smiled her odd little half smile at Eddie as if she knew all of their secrets. "I have a wonderful surprise," she told the class in her thick Transylvanian accent. "Our new band teacher has chosen our class to perform at the upcoming Fall Festival. He's asked for extra practice time and I have agreed."

A few kids in the class clapped, but Eddie and Liza slumped down in their

129

seats. "So much for staying away from him," Liza muttered.

Mrs. Jeepers flashed her green eyes and continued. "Mr. Belgrave has also informed me that a very special surprise guest will be performing with you at the festival."

"Who is it?" Melody asked with her hand raised.

"I cannot tell you that," Mrs. Jeepers said, rubbing her brooch. "If I told you, it would ruin the surprise."

"That's okay," Eddie said. "I don't like surprises anyway."

Mrs. Jeepers looked at Eddie and rubbed her brooch. "I will give you one clue," she said.

"What?" Howie asked.

"The surprise performer will play the tuba," Mrs. Jeepers said in her strange accent.

Eddie heard a loud noise and looked around. Liza had fallen out of her chair

130

and was sitting on the floor with books scattered all around her.

Mrs. Jeepers rushed over. "Are you all right?" she asked, helping Liza back into her seat.

"I . . . I . . . I think so," Liza stuttered. "I just felt funny there for a moment."

"I know what's wrong," Eddie told Mrs. Jeepers. "Liza hit her funny bones the wrong way."

Liza looked at Eddie. "It's bones, all right," she said, "but there is nothing funny about it."

That afternoon at recess, the four friends gathered under the big oak tree on the playground. Liza was about to cry. "Mr. Belgrave is going to have Claude play at the Fall Festival!"

"Don't be ridiculous," Melody told her.

"Who else can play the tuba?" Liza asked. "I don't want to play in the festival if I have to play with a skeleton."

"Don't worry about it," Eddie said. "I've figured out a way to get to the bottom of this bony business."

"What are you going to do?" Howie asked.

"I'll explain everything," Eddie told them. Even though the rest of the third-graders were screaming on the jungle gym, Eddie was careful to whisper his plan. Howie, Melody, and Liza leaned close so they could hear.

133

Liza shivered. "I hope you know what you're doing. If I hear Claude playing the tuba one more time, I think I'll turn into a skeleton myself."

9

Night School

That evening, dark storm clouds hung low over Bailey City and lightning streaked across the sky. A cold autumn wind rattled the branches of the oak tree, sending withered leaves floating to the ground near the four huddled friends. Liza pulled her coat tight about her before she faced Eddie. "Are you sure this is a good idea?" she asked.

Melody nodded. "We could get into trouble."

"*Big* trouble," Howie added.

Eddie glanced at the dark windows of Bailey Elementary. "We'll be in bigger trouble if we don't. Besides, this is the perfect time."

"How do you figure that?" Melody asked.

135

"Listen," Eddie said.

Howie, Melody, and Liza stood as still as statues. They heard muffled music floating from the empty building. "Someone is playing the tuba," Eddie said, "and I think it's Claude."

Without another word, Eddie stalked across the playground and pulled open the side door to the school. "How did you know it'd be open?" Howie asked.

"I knew the janitor would still be here," Eddie whispered as he went in the door. Once inside, the four friends stopped long enough to let their eyes get used to the dark hall. Thunder made the windows rattle and drifting clouds cast long shadows on the black-and-white floor.

"We should have brought a flashlight," Liza whimpered.

"I have a flashlight," Howie said, reaching into his pocket.

"No," Eddie said softly. "We have to

surprise him. A flashlight would be like an invitation to a funeral. Our funeral. Now, let's go."

Carefully, Eddie led his friends down the hall. Melody walked beside Eddie with Howie close behind. Liza took her time. She didn't like the darkness or the music echoing through the deserted school. The tuba notes sounded like the beating heart of a monster and they grew louder and louder as the four friends got closer to the old science lab. They were almost there when . . .

Wham! Liza found herself sprawled on the floor. She screamed just to make sure she was still alive. She had been so busy peering over her shoulder that she hadn't seen the swinging door sticking out into the hall. Instead of walking around it like her friends, she had crashed right into the door, slamming it shut.

Everyone froze.

"Shhhh!" Eddie warned. But it was too late. The music stopped, filling the halls of Bailey Elementary with a deadly silence.

Melody grabbed Liza's arm and pulled her into a nearby janitor's closet. "She didn't mean to do it," Melody whispered to Eddie as the kids hid.

"She should have watched where she was going," Eddie snapped.

Liza sniffed and wiped a tear from her cheek while Howie peeked out the closet door toward the band room. "Maybe he didn't hear us," Howie suggested. "The door is still closed, nobody left."

"Of course nobody heard," Eddie muttered. "Claude has 'no body.'"

Melody patted Liza on the shoulder. "We should forget this boneheaded plan and get home," Melody told Eddie, "before Liza's nose starts bleeding."

Liza nodded. Her nose often bled when she was upset, and she was plenty nervous right now. "I hear Claude coming to get us!" she whimpered.

Howie slapped his forehead. "That was just me cracking my knuckles. Next, you'll think Melody's chattering teeth is Claude doing a tap dance!"

"You still don't believe Claude is alive, do you?" Eddie asked his friend.

"Of course not," Howie said. "I don't believe in ghouls or zombies or living, breathing skeletons."

"Then you won't mind walking down that hall and taking a look in the band room?" Eddie asked.

Howie peeked out of the closet again and down the long, dark hallway. It looked like a big black mouth waiting to swallow him up, but he wasn't about to let his friends see him scared.

"I'll go," Howie told him. "But you have

to come with me. And bring the flashlight."

Eddie barely nodded. "Let's do it." They slipped out of the closet with Melody and Liza right behind them.

There was no music now. The only sound was the thunder rumbling over the Red River. Howie drew a deep breath before pulling open the band room door. There, glowing in the dim flashlight, was Claude and he was holding the tuba.

"Run!" Howie screamed. At least, he tried to scream but it sounded more like a bullfrog croaking under water. But his friends knew what he meant, and they tore down the hall like they were racing lightning.

"This way!" Liza screamed. She led her friends around a corner and toward an exit sign. Heavy footsteps echoed behind them.

"Hurry!" Melody gasped. "Before that skeleton makes mincemeat out of us."

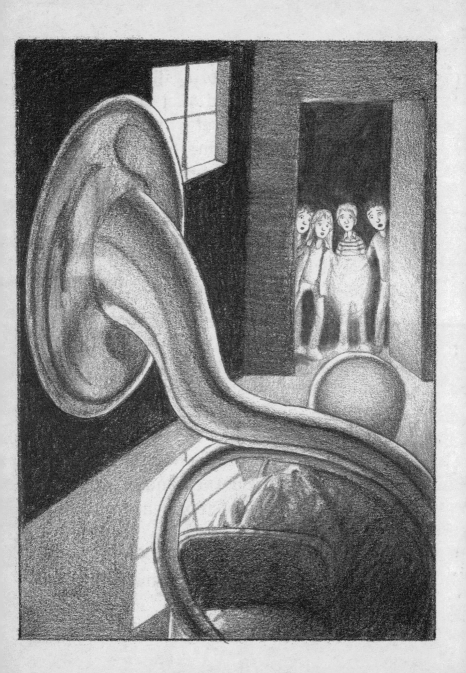

Liza crashed against the door, frantically pushing the handle. "It's locked," she cried.

The four friends backed against the locked door and faced the long, dark corridor. "We have to find another way out!" Howie sputtered.

"It's too late," Eddie said as the heavy footsteps came closer.

10

Skull

"Oh my gosh," Liza squealed before ducking behind Melody. "I see his skull!"

In a flash of lightning, the kids did see a skull. But they also saw round glasses and an egg-shaped body.

"Principal Davis!" Howie said in relief. "What are you doing here?"

Principal Davis scratched his bald head. "I was going to ask you the same question. After all, school was over hours ago."

Eddie was used to fibbing to the principal. "Oh, we came by to get our spelling books so we could study."

Principal Davis nodded his head slowly. "I'm glad that you wanted to study, but it's too late now. Go home and go to bed. Get plenty of rest. Don't forget the Fall Festival is tomorrow."

"Yes, sir," Melody said, eager to get out of the school.

Principal Davis pulled a ring of keys from his pocket to unlock the door. "Don't let me catch you in here again so late," he warned.

"No, sir," Eddie said innocently as the four kids trotted out the door.

But Liza couldn't leave without asking Principal Davis a question. "Did you hear music?" she asked.

"Music?" Principal Davis said, smiling. "Perhaps you heard my radio. I just love listening to band music. The sound of a brass instrument just sends chills up my spine."

"Mine too," Eddie muttered when Principal Davis closed the door.

Thunder rumbled as the kids gathered under the oak tree. "Let's get home," Liza said. "It's going to storm any minute."

"But first, we have to figure out how to

save the school from Claude," Eddie told his friends.

Melody pulled her jacket tighter. "You heard Principal Davis. It was just his radio we heard."

Eddie shook his head. "I don't think so."

"A radio makes perfect sense," Melody insisted.

"I'm beginning to wonder," Howie said. "Even Mrs. Jeepers said it was tuba music. And don't forget we saw Claude holding the tuba with our own eyes."

"And he was glowing!" Liza shuddered. "I know it was him chasing us. There's no telling what would have happened if Principal Davis hadn't come along."

Howie nodded. "This is getting stranger and stranger. I think we need to get to the bottom of this whole thing."

"Before Bailey City has skeletons walking the streets," Eddie agreed. The four kids started walking slowly home, trying to think of a plan. But when a loud moaning sound came from the school, they jumped.

"The tuba!" Liza screeched. The four friends ran down the street.

11

Believe It or Not

"Pssst!" Howie peeked around from behind the oak tree the next morning before school, motioning for Eddie and Liza to join him. "I've figured out a solution to our skeleton scare," he told his friends. "We don't have a thing to worry about."

Howie reached into a brown paper bag and pulled out a long knotted string. "This is for you," he told Liza. "And here's one for Eddie."

Eddie slapped his forehead. "Great! I'm supposed to protect myself from a killer skeleton with a piece of twine! What am I going to do? Floss his knuckles?"

Howie didn't laugh. "Don't worry, Bone Brains, there's more. Much more." But before he could pull anything else from his bag of tricks, Melody looked around the huge tree trunk.

"What are you guys up to?" she asked. "You're going to be late for class if you don't hurry."

Liza grabbed Melody's coat sleeve and pulled her around the oak tree. "Howie has a plan to protect us from Claude."

Melody giggled. "A marshmallow could protect us from that stack of bones."

"If you don't believe in living skeletons, then you won't mind wearing this," Howie told her. He pulled a tiny paper jack-o'-lantern out of his crinkled bag.

Melody sat down on the brown grass and giggled. "Why would I want to wear an itty-bitty pumpkin?"

"Remember what Mrs. Jeepers said? Jack-o'-lanterns are supposed to ward off evil spirits," Howie said matter-of-factly.

"They haven't gotten rid of Eddie yet," Melody kidded. "And Claude is nothing to be afraid of compared to Eddie!"

Howie stared hard at Melody. "This is no joking matter. Jack-o'-lanterns were originally used to get rid of dead spirits, and I can't think of anything deader than a skeleton."

"But Claude is just the remains of an old science kit," Melody argued.

"Old science kits don't do bone dances on kids' backs," Eddie disagreed. "I think we'd better listen to Howie."

Howie handed the paper jack-o'-lantern and string to Melody. "After all, it won't hurt to wear this around your neck," he said, "even if you don't believe. And if what Mrs. Jeepers said is true, it'll put a muffler on Claude. It'll prove that he's alive!"

"The only thing this proves is that you have a cracked skull yourself," Melody told Howie. But she threaded the twine through a hole in the pumpkin stem and put the homemade necklace over her neck. Liza and Eddie did the same.

Liza's eyes grew big. "But what if Mrs. Jeepers sees them? I don't think she wants jack-o'-lanterns in the classroom."

Howie nodded. "I remembered. I made them small so we can hide them under our shirts. Now, let's go."

Once inside the classroom, the four friends slid into their seats and started their day's work. Mrs. Jeepers was known for giving more assignments than any other teacher at Bailey Elementary. It was hard to work, knowing that the Fall Festival was just a few hours away, but the third-graders opened their books and got busy anyway. Nobody dared upset Mrs. Jeepers.

They were halfway done with their math when Howie kicked Melody in the shin. "Did you notice something?" he whispered.

Melody glanced at Mrs. Jeepers to make

sure she wasn't looking, but the third-grade teacher was busy helping Carey multiply three numbers together. Melody shook her head to answer Howie.

"It's quiet," he told her.

"So?" Melody shrugged. "Mrs. Jeepers's room is always quiet."

"The rest of the school is silent, too," Howie pointed out. "There's no tuba music!"

Melody's mouth dropped open, but Howie didn't notice. "I was right," he hissed. "The jack-o'-lanterns are working." He smiled and pulled out his tiny necklace to prove his point.

But Howie's face turned a shade of green when long white fingers reached from behind him and slowly circled his wrist.

Mrs. Jeepers stood in front of Howie. "I do not want these in my classroom," she said in her thick accent. "There are

154

many other decorations of the fall season. Please take those necklaces off." Mrs. Jeepers touched her green brooch and flashed her eyes at the other children. Slowly Melody, Liza, Howie, and Eddie gave their necklaces to their teacher.

12

Doomed

"Now what are we going to do?" Liza moaned at the lunch table. "The Fall Festival is less than an hour away and we don't have our jack-o'-lanterns. Mrs. Jeepers locked them in her drawer."

"Maybe we could make some more?" Howie suggested.

"There's no time," Liza whimpered.

Eddie shot his straw wrapper at Howie. "If Bone Head here hadn't been showing off, we'd have been okay."

"We have nothing to worry about," Melody defended Howie. "After all, it's been quiet all day."

Eddie looked hopeful. "Maybe old 'Claude without a bod' knows we're on to him and decided to keep his mouth shut."

The kids nodded and bit into their pizza slices without another thought to skeleton bones, alive or dead. But as they lined up to go to the festival, Claude was on their minds again. Long, sad tuba notes echoed down the halls of Bailey Elementary.

"Oh, no!" Liza cried. "It's Claude. Just in time for the festival!"

The kids had no choice but to file into the gymnasium behind Mrs. Jeepers. There, sitting on the stage, for everyone to see, was Claude. He was holding the tuba and he was smiling!

Mrs. Jeepers turned to her students and smiled. "Good luck, ladies and gentlemen. You are the first to perform. You may go on the stage now."

Liza shook her head and hid behind Melody. "There's no way I'm going on that stage."

Mrs. Jeepers smiled her strange little half smile. "No need to be afraid. Every-

one has had stage fright from time to time. Let me help you." She grabbed Liza's hand and pulled her up onto the stage with the rest of the class following. Mrs. Jeepers sat Liza right in front of Claude and patted her on the shoulder.

"I think my nose is going to bleed," Liza whined.

"Do not worry," Mrs. Jeepers said as she stepped to the side of the stage. "You will do fine."

Mr. Belgrave stood in front of the class and tapped his conductor's baton on a music stand. The students picked up their instruments and began playing "The Bailey Elementary March." The students played their best and Mr. Belgrave smiled a big yellow-toothed smile.

Halfway through the song, low sad notes came from behind Liza's chair. Liza gulped and almost dropped her saxophone. When the song was over, everyone in the audience clapped and cheered.

Mrs. Jeepers smiled her odd little half smile and nodded. Liza smiled back and bowed with the rest of the class. Then very slowly, she turned to look behind her. What she saw almost made her faint.

13

Two Bald Heads

Instead of one bald head behind Liza, there were two. One belonged to Claude and the other one belonged to Principal Davis. Both of them were smiling, but now Principal Davis had the tuba wrapped around him.

"How did you like my surprise?" Principal Davis asked Liza. "I bet you didn't know your old principal could toot a horn."

Liza shook her head with relief but Eddie stepped up beside her. "I knew it was you playing the tuba all along," Eddie bragged.

"You did not!" Melody put her hands on her hips and looked at Eddie. "You thought Claude was playing."

Eddie's face turned bright red to match

his hair. "I did not!" he lied. "After all, skeletons don't play tubas."

Mrs. Jeepers came up beside Eddie. "I did not know you were so interested in skeletons," she told him. "You will be delighted with our new science unit."

Eddie shook his head. "Science has never delighted me before."

Mrs. Jeepers touched her green brooch and smiled. "You will like this," she said with certainty.

"What will we be studying?" Melody asked.

"The human skeleton," Mrs. Jeepers said.

Eddie didn't say anything as everyone around him laughed. But he gulped when he thought he saw Claude wink at him.

Cupid
Doesn't Flip
Hamburgers

To our special valentines: Steve and Eric
                              — MTJ and DD

1

St. Valentine's Day

"Pink lace and frills! This is girls' stuff," Eddie complained, crumpling the paper valentine he was making into a wad. He glanced around the classroom to make sure his teacher, Mrs. Jeepers, wasn't watching. After all, most kids thought she was a vampire, and didn't dare do anything to make her green eyes flash.

Luckily for Eddie, Mrs. Jeepers was busy at the door talking to Principal Davis. Eddie eyed his target. A head full of bouncy yellow curls was just three seats away. With careful aim, he let his ruined valentine soar across the aisle. *Smack!* It landed right in the middle of Carey's blonde head.

"Bingo!" Eddie mouthed when Carey

twisted around to give him a mean look.

"I bet you won't get a single valentine," Carey blurted out. Unfortunately, she was so mad, she forgot to whisper. The class gasped when Mrs. Jeepers slowly turned around and flashed her eyes at Carey.

"I am surprised to hear such a terrible insult," Mrs. Jeepers said in her strange Transylvanian accent.

"But, Eddie threw — " Carey started to say.

"Enough!" Mrs. Jeepers interrupted and rubbed her green brooch. "Valentine's Day is a time to show people we appreciate them. You must apologize for being rude."

Carey's face turned bright red. "But . . ."

"Apologize," Mrs. Jeepers insisted.

The rest of the class watched as Carey faced Eddie. "I'm sorry," she muttered through clenched teeth. Then she turned

171

around and stared at the half-made valentine on her own desk.

Eddie smiled his sweetest smile until Mrs. Jeepers went back to talking with Principal Davis. Then he giggled as he pulled the eraser off his pencil and flicked it.

Carey flinched when the eraser popped her on the back. But she wasn't about to turn around and get in trouble again, and Eddie knew it.

Melody sat behind Eddie. "You'd better stop it," she warned. "Before Mrs. Jeepers catches you."

But Eddie was having too much fun. As long as Mrs. Jeepers was busy, he was going to keep it up. He was just about to send a broken crayon hurtling toward Carey when Mrs. Jeepers looked at the class and cleared her throat. Eddie quickly sat up straight and smiled sweetly.

"It is time for us to go to the cafeteria,"

Mrs. Jeepers said. Then she smiled an odd little half-smile. "Today, we will meet our new cook, Mrs. Rosenbloom."

Half the class groaned, but Liza raised her hand. "Maybe we should give Mrs. Rosenbloom a valentine, too."

"What a wonderful idea," Mrs. Jeepers said. "Please line up and bring one of your cards." Most of the kids rushed to line up, but Eddie, Liza, Melody, and Howie waited to be last.

"That was a dopey idea," Eddie told Liza.

"You're just mad because you didn't get any valentine cards made," Howie interrupted.

Melody nodded. "You were too busy bothering Carey."

"And she's never going to forgive you," Liza added. "Carey has never been in trouble before."

"I don't care about her or valentines," Eddie said, shaking his head as they headed for the lunchroom. "But I do care about my empty stomach. I'm hungry. We always have the same old slop in the cafeteria."

"Maybe the new cook will be different," Liza said.

Eddie shook his head. "That just means we'll have new slop."

"Eddie, you should give her a chance. She may be a really good cook," Melody said as they walked into the cafeteria.

"It'll be the first good cook at Ba — " Eddie said, but he stopped at the entrance of the cafeteria.

"What in the world happened?" Howie asked.

2

Explosion

"It looks like a card store exploded in here," Howie said, looking around the cafeteria. All sizes of red, pink, and white paper hearts were everywhere the kids looked. Hearts were plastered to the walls, hanging from the ceiling, and even stuck onto the garbage cans.

Melody giggled. "They must have had a five-for-one heart sale."

"Five dumb decorations for the price of one," Eddie said. "This place looks stupid."

"I think it's pretty," Liza said. "After all, Valentine's Day is less than a week away."

Eddie rolled his eyes. "Valentine's Day is for three year olds who don't have anything better to do."

"Valentine's Day is for telling people you like them," Melody told him.

"Or that you love them," Liza giggled.

"That's disgusting," Eddie said.

"There's nothing disgusting about *love*," said a voice from beside them. "But you'll find that out soon enough."

Eddie looked up and gulped. In front of him was the biggest red dress he'd ever seen and it was being worn by the biggest woman he'd ever seen. Almost everything about her was big and red, from her big, bright red lips to her fluffy reddish-blonde hair. Even the heart button on her apron and her dangling heart earrings were big and red.

But when she grabbed Eddie's cheeks, he noticed that her fingernails were painted hot pink with little white arrows on them. "You're just the cutest little thing," the woman said as she squeezed Eddie's cheeks. "I just *love* your red hair. What a cutie pie!"

"You must be Mrs. Rosenbloom, the new cook," Liza said. "Welcome to Bailey Elementary." Liza held out her valentine to the big woman.

"Why, thank you, sugar." Mrs. Rosenbloom smiled and gave Liza a bear hug. "I just know I'm going to *love* it here!"

"We hope so," Howie said politely. "Did you do the decorating?"

"Why, yes." Mrs. Rosenbloom blushed. "I just *love* Valentine's Day. But that's enough talking. Come eat."

The four kids followed the rest of their class through the lunch line and picked up their trays.

"I've never seen so much red in my life," Eddie said. Everything on their lunch trays was red. There was heart-shaped meatloaf covered with ketchup and a tomato slice in a heart shape. Each tray had a slice of red apple with a heart-shaped blob of cherry Jell-O. There were even red straws for the milk.

"I think this lady fell off the old holiday wagon before her brain was fully cooked," Eddie said when they sat down with their trays. "She's gone heart crazy."

"I think it's nice," Liza said. "It sure beats the tuna surprise we usually have on Mondays."

"Baked bowling balls would beat that," Melody agreed after taking a bite of the Jell-O. "This stuff may be red, but it's good."

"There's nothing good about overdosing on red," Eddie said. "That new cook may need surgery to remove all these hearts. And I'm just the doctor to handle it."

"Who are you?" Howie laughed. "Doctor Love?"

"Doctor Meanie would be more like it," Liza said. "Don't go bothering Mrs. Rosenbloom. She's nice."

Eddie smiled. "Would I bother a sweet lady like her?"

His three friends all nodded their heads yes. Eddie had a reputation for causing mischief. But none of the four kids noticed Mrs. Rosenbloom standing nearby. She was touching her heart button and she was smiling.

3

Love Bug

"There's that prissy Carey kissing up to Mrs. Rosenbloom," Eddie pointed as he slurped the last of his cherry Jell-O.

"No fair!" Melody said. "Mrs. Rosenbloom is giving Carey a heart button and a cookie."

"Carey gets everything." Liza sighed. Carey's dad owned the Bailey City Bank. Carey was always bringing new toys to school or bragging about something her dad bought her.

"I'll make sure she gets a hard time," Eddie said with an evil grin. He grabbed his half-empty lunch tray and headed for Carey. Mrs. Rosenbloom finished pinning the button on Carey and spun her around to face Eddie.

"Why, hello, Eddie," Carey said with a

mouth full of cookie. "Fancy meeting you here."

"Yeah, it's a miracle," Eddie said. "Would you like my apple slice?"

"I'd *love* it!" Carey said, snapping it off Eddie's tray. "But, then, I'd adore anything of yours!" She batted her eyelashes at Eddie before nibbling on the apple. Eddie gave her a funny look, then rushed back to his seat.

"I can't believe you gave Carey your apple," Melody said. "I thought you hated her."

"I can't stand her," Eddie agreed. "I dropped it on the floor. That's why I gave it to her."

"That wasn't very nice," Liza said.

"Speaking of nice. Do you see the way Carey keeps looking at you?" Howie asked Eddie. The four kids turned to see Carey tossing her blonde hair and fluttering her eyebrows in their direction.

Melody giggled. "I think she's been bitten by the love bug!"

"You guys are crazy." Eddie shook his head and looked at Carey. She smiled and blew him a kiss!

Eddie splashed through a mud puddle on his way across the playground the next morning. Melody, Liza, and Howie were huddled under a huge oak tree comparing answers to their math homework.

"Number thirteen has to be three hundred and forty-two hearts," Melody was explaining.

Howie shook his head. "You weren't supposed to add. You should have subtracted."

Liza frowned. "I multiplied! What did you get for the answer, Eddie?"

Eddie looked at his friends like they'd just sprouted broccoli out of their ears. "What homework?"

Melody rolled her eyes. "You'll never make it out of third grade unless you do the homework."

"I'll help you," a sweet voice interrupted.

The four friends turned to face Carey. She winked at Eddie. "I have all the answers and mine are always right."

Eddie kicked his foot into the mud, splattering Carey's pink boots with brown goo. "I don't need any help," he said, "especially from you." Then he stomped toward the school.

"But I don't mind helping *you*," Carey insisted as she grabbed his elbow. "I brought you something, too."

Eddie skidded to a stop. "You're trying to get me back for yesterday's paper wad. You'd give me the wrong answers just to get me in trouble."

"Don't be silly," Carey said, batting her eyelashes at him. "Here, this proves I'm not mad at you." She reached inside her bookbag and pulled out a red rose. "I even snipped the thorns off so you won't get pricked."

Eddie backed away and bumped into Melody.

"It's not every day a guy gets a flower from his girlfriend," Melody said with a giggle.

"Carey is not my girlfriend!" Eddie yelled as he ran into the school.

Carey sighed and flipped her golden curls behind her ears. "Poor Eddie. I'll just have to try harder."

"Try harder to do what?" Liza asked from behind Melody.

Carey looked at Melody, Howie, and Liza as if she were going to tell them the answers to next week's science test. But then she shook her head and followed Eddie into the school. "Never mind. You just wouldn't understand."

"Something strange is going on at Bailey Elementary," Melody said.

Howie nodded. "I never dreamed I'd see the day when Carey was nice to Eddie."

"It's almost like she's in love with him," Liza said softly.

"Don't be silly," Melody said. "Godzilla is more lovable than Eddie." The three friends nodded and went inside the school building. Once inside, the kids stopped dead in their tracks.

"Maybe Liza's right," Howie said.

Melody started laughing so hard, she snorted through her nose. "It looks like Carey has Eddie cornered."

Sure enough, Carey had grabbed Eddie's notebook at the water fountain. "I'd *love* to carry your books," she was telling him.

Eddie tugged as hard as he could, but Carey wouldn't let go. "Give it to me!" Eddie jerked his notebook one last time, tearing the cover in half. "Now look what you've done!" Eddie yelled.

"I'm sorry," Carey said. "I'll get you a new one."

Eddie gave her a look and dashed into the classroom. Melody, Howie, and Liza followed and started teasing Eddie.

"It looks like Carey's fallen for you," Howie whispered.

Eddie took a pencil out of his desk and shook his head. "She's just trying to make me mad."

"It looks like love to me." Melody nodded toward the doorway. Carey stood there straightening the heart pin on her pink sweater. Then she strode to Eddie and paused beside his desk. She smiled and put a chocolate kiss on his desk. She winked and walked to her own desk.

From behind him, Eddie heard Melody giggle as she started singing. "Eddie and Carey, sitting in a tree, K-I-S-S-I-N-G . . . first comes love . . ."

But before she could sing any more, Eddie took the candy kiss and flung it over his shoulder. It landed with a definite *thunk* on Melody's forehead.

4

Lovesick

For the first time in his life, Eddie kept his eyes on his schoolwork. He didn't actually do much of it, but he kept his eyes on his paper anyway. He didn't want to look up and catch Carey staring at him again. That's what had happened right in the middle of the science experiment. She'd smiled and winked at him. Then she blew him a kiss. Eddie had spilled an entire test tube of saltwater in his lap.

Then Howie made kissing noises. "Quit it," Eddie warned. "Or I'll smack you right across the face."

By lunchtime, Eddie was ready to leave school and Bailey City, too. Melody grabbed his shoulder. "Looks like you've fallen in love with the smartest girl in class," she teased.

"She must not be that smart," Howie interrupted. "Not if she likes Eddie!"

"That's enough," Eddie sputtered. "There is something very fishy about this."

"I'll say." Melody laughed. "It's fishy that anyone would bring you red roses and candy kisses."

Liza nodded. "All you deserve are thorns and spinach."

Eddie turned his back on his friends and hurried to lunch. The whole school had turned against him. Everyone that is, except Carey. And that was even worse.

Red and pink hearts were still all over the cafeteria. Eddie had already had his fill of Valentine's Day nonsense. He grabbed his tray of a heart-shaped sandwich, a pink-frosted cupcake, and cherry-flavored juice and headed for the corner table. He didn't speak when Liza, Howie, and Melody sat down. Instead, he

kept his eyes on the new cook. There was something about her that bothered him.

He watched her smile and hand out trays of pink and red goop. But Eddie stopped chewing his heart-shaped sandwich when Ben came through the line. Ben was the biggest bully in the fourth grade. Eddie got some of his best ideas from watching Ben. Eddie couldn't wait to see how Ben handled the new cook.

"Why so grumpy?" Mrs. Rosenbloom put her hands on her wide waist and laughed. "You need something to sweeten up your insides." Then she pulled a huge cookie from off a top shelf. It was smothered in icing and little pieces of red candy. Eddie licked his lips as Ben wolfed down the cookie.

With his hands full, Ben couldn't stop Mrs. Rosenbloom from pinning a heart button onto his shirt. "That ought to do the trick," Mrs. Rosenbloom said as Ben walked away still chomping on the cookie.

Eddie's eyes widened when he saw the button. It was identical to Carey's.

Eddie smiled when Ben stopped beside Isabell Hart. "Look," Eddie said to his friends. "Ben's going to let prissy Issy have it."

The four kids watched. But Ben didn't spit or burp or tease Issy. Instead, he sat down beside her and shared his cookie.

Eddie drummed his fingers on the table. Something was wrong, really wrong, but he couldn't put his finger on it. And then it came to him. He slapped the table with his hand, sending spoons and forks clattering to the floor. "I've got it!" he blurted.

"Got what?" Melody asked. "The chicken pox?"

Eddie ignored Melody. "I've got the answer to everything."

"Great," Howie said. "Then you can take my science test for me."

"No," Eddie snapped. "I know why Carey and Ben are acting like lovesick slugs."

"Why?" Liza asked.

Eddie looked at his friends and kept his voice low. "Everything was normal until yesterday."

"Nothing is ever normal at Bailey Elementary," Melody interrupted.

Eddie nodded. "But until then, Carey

and Ben were the same old pests."

"What are you getting at?" Howie asked.

"It's the work of Mrs. Rosenbloom," Eddie explained. "She's invaded Bailey Elementary and she's armed with love potions!"

5

Love Potions

Howie choked on his heart-shaped sandwich and Melody laughed so hard, she spit milk onto the table. Even Liza got caught in a fit of giggles.

"There are no such things as love potions," Melody told Eddie while she mopped up her milk using a red heart napkin.

"Mrs. Rosenbloom is just spreading good cheer," Liza said. "There's nothing wrong with being nice."

"There is if you don't want to be nice," Eddie snapped. "Mrs. Rosenbloom is ruining Bailey Elementary. Everyone is turning into gushy, oogle-eyed love-struck twirps!"

"You make Mrs. Rosenbloom sound like Cupid," Melody said.

197

"Who?" Eddie and Liza asked together.

Howie pointed to a picture on the wall. "Cupid is the fat little baby who shoots arrows at people. Whoever gets hit with an arrow falls in love."

Eddie shrugged. "Who knows? Maybe she is Cupid. She's not a baby, but you have to admit, she is pretty chubby."

His three friends started laughing again. Eddie glared at them and stood up to leave. "You wait and see. Before long, everyone will be a lovey-dovey goodie two-shoes and it'll all be Mrs. Rosenbloom's fault!" Eddie left his giggling friends and threw his trash in the garbage can. When he turned to leave, his view was blocked by a huge red wall with lacy pockets. He slowly looked up, right into the grinning face of Mrs. Rosenbloom.

"Howdy," Mrs. Rosenbloom said. "It looks like you've lost your best friend. I bet a big old sugar cookie would fill your day with sunshine."

"N-n-no thanks," Eddie stuttered and backed away. He bumped right into Carey.

Carey smiled and batted her eyelashes at Eddie. "How about a chocolate kiss?" she asked.

Eddie looked at Mrs. Rosenbloom and at Carey. Then he did the only thing he could do. He ran. He darted past a very surprised Mrs. Rosenbloom. He skidded around a corner and raced back to the classroom as fast as he could.

Eddie's heart was still thumping when the rest of the class quietly filed into the third-grade room.

Melody whispered to Eddie, "Mrs. Jeepers will turn you into bat bait when she finds out you were running in the cafeteria."

Howie nodded. "I bet Mrs. Rosenbloom is telling her how rude you were."

"I wasn't being rude," Eddie argued. "I was running for my life."

Liza laughed. "You were running from a sugar cookie."

"A cookie filled with love potion," Eddie said.

"You're going to need some of that love potion to save you from Mrs. Jeepers," Melody warned. Their teacher didn't allow her students to be rude. The kids got quiet as Mrs. Jeepers came into the room and looked at Eddie.

But Mrs. Jeepers didn't flash her eyes at Eddie and she didn't rub her mysterious brooch like she usually did when she was angry. Instead, she smiled. Her cheeks were flushed rosy-red, instead of their usual chalk-white color.

"What's wrong with her?" Liza whispered. "Do you think she's sick?"

No one had time to answer, because a loud knock at the door interrupted them. Principal Davis opened the door, wearing a huge heart pin. He held out a sugar cookie and smiled at Mrs. Jeepers. "You

201

forgot your cookie," he said. "So I brought it to you."

Mrs. Jeepers' face blushed to a deep shade of purple. She took the half-eaten cookie from Principal Davis. "Why, thank you," she said. "I do *love* sugar cookies."

Principal Davis smiled and waved good-bye. "I was happy to bring it."

Mrs. Jeepers closed the door and faced her class. What Eddie saw made him drop his math book. Mrs. Jeepers was wearing a heart pin, too.

6

Button Attack

"Don't you guys get it?" Eddie yelled. "She's taking over our school!"

"Eddie, you have the craziest imagination," Liza told him. Liza, Melody, Eddie, and Howie were all gathered under their favorite oak tree after school.

Melody agreed. "I've heard people say that love is war — "

"It's the attack of the killer buttons!" Eddie interrupted. "Everybody who wears one and eats a sugar cookie goes love crazy!"

"That's ridiculous!" Liza said. "Just because Mrs. Jeepers is wearing a heart button is nothing to get excited about. After all, she wears a green brooch every day."

"But it's not every day that she acts like

a lovesick puppy," Eddie pointed out.

Howie leaned against the oak tree. "She did act stranger than usual. At recess time, she actually was humming a song."

"It was a love song," Melody said. "And during math, she drew hearts on the board! She's never done that before."

"See!" Eddie yelled. "I told you something like this was going to happen, but you wouldn't believe me. We have to do something before it's too late."

"Hold on just a minute," Melody said. "There's nothing wrong with drawing hearts or humming love songs. The world would probably be a lot better if everyone was a little more loving."

"Melody is right. Just think what it would be like if everyone loved everyone else," Liza said.

Eddie started to say something, but he didn't get the chance. Carey came up behind him and put her hands over his eyes.

"Guess who?" Carey said.

"My worst nightmare!" Eddie yelled and pushed Carey's hands away.

Carey winked and grabbed Eddie's hand. "Oh, Eddie. You are so funny. Would you like to walk me home?"

"No!" Eddie hollered and pulled away. "No! No!" Eddie looked at Howie, Liza, and Melody. "See! Just look what that cook has done. She's taken two perfectly good enemies and spoiled them."

Carey batted her eyelashes at Eddie. "We could never be enemies. I like you too much. As a matter of fact, I lo — "

"Aaahhh!" Eddie screamed. "This has gone too far! I've got to do something!" Then he ran out of the playground and didn't stop until he was safe at home.

Carey looked at Melody, Howie, and Liza. "He's playing hard to get," Carey said. "I think I'll bake him some sugar cookies."

The next morning, Eddie came to school and didn't say a word. He didn't say anything when Howie said hello, and he just put his head down when Carey offered him a big fat red cookie and gave him a new pink notebook. He didn't even comment when Mrs. Jeepers came in wearing a bright red dress with a white rose in her hair.

"I saw Principal Davis give her that rose," Liza whispered. "I think they're in love. Mrs. Jeepers has probably been lonely since her husband died."

"Maybe you were right about those buttons and cookies," Howie muttered. Eddie didn't say a word, but he did notice that Mrs. Jeepers was still wearing her heart button.

Finally at lunch, Eddie spoke. "Whatever happens, don't eat one of those heart cookies or wear one of those buttons."

Liza rolled her eyes. "You still don't believe that Cupid nonsense, do you? Just look at Mrs. Rosenbloom. She looks perfectly innocent."

The four friends looked through the open kitchen door. Mrs. Rosenbloom was there in a bright red dress with a white apron and a big white hat. She was busy cooking heart-shaped hamburgers on the grill. Every once in a while, she would toss one of the burgers. The hamburger

would swirl through the air and Mrs. Rosenbloom would catch it on a plate.

"I've never seen Cupid flipping hamburgers before," Melody said.

"Maybe she's the first one," Eddie said. "After all, Cupids have to eat, too. That's how they get so fat."

"You're crazy," Liza said. "Besides, those cookies that she baked look good. Just look at those yummy red sprinkles on top. I have to get one." Liza stood up to go into the kitchen and Melody followed.

"I'm going to get one of those cute buttons," Melody added.

Eddie shook his head at Howie and took a bite of his heart-shaped hamburger. "Somebody has to cure Bailey School kids of this lovesickness. And it will have to be me."

7

Love Is War

Melody closed her eyes and swallowed. "This is the best cookie I've ever sunk my teeth into."

Liza nodded and licked a few sprinkles off her red cookie. "I just *love* them!"

Melody giggled, and she and Liza walked back toward their seats in the lunchroom. "But nothing is sweeter than Howie. He's so cute and smart."

"I'm glad he's my friend," Liza told her. "I think he likes me better than you."

"Your brain is as mushy as oatmeal," Melody snapped. "Howie likes me best."

Liza sniffed and touched Melody's arm. "He does not."

"Does too!" Melody pushed her best friend.

Liza fell against the wall and slid to the

floor. "Look what you did!" Liza shrieked.

"It's your own fault," Melody yelled. The rest of the kids in the cafeteria fell silent. Melody and Liza had been best friends since kindergarten. They hardly ever had fights.

Howie and Eddie stared at Liza and Melody. "What's gotten into them?" Eddie asked.

Howie shrugged. "We'd better help them out. If Mrs. Jeepers finds out they were fighting, she'll send them to Principal Davis' office."

Howie and Eddie rushed across the crowded cafeteria. Without thinking, Howie held out his hand to help Liza up.

Liza smiled sweetly and batted her eyelashes. Then she gently placed her hand in Howie's. "See," she told Melody. "Howie likes me best."

Howie's mouth dropped open and his face turned as red as the sprinkles on

Mrs. Rosenbloom's cookies. "I never said that!" Howie sputtered.

Liza squeezed his hand and winked. "It's okay, Howie. I like you, too!"

Howie pulled his hand away and took three steps back. "What's wrong with you, Liza?" he asked. "Are you sick?"

Eddie stepped between Liza and Howie. "Liza's sick, all right. Lovesick."

"Am not!" Liza blurted. "Melody's the one who's sick. She thinks Howie likes her better than me! Tell her the truth, Howie!"

Howie looked at Liza, then at Melody. If he said he liked Liza, Melody would get mad. If he said he liked Melody, Liza would get upset and her nose would bleed. "I like you both," he finally admitted. "We're friends."

"You can't like us both," Melody snapped. "You have to pick who you like best." She put her hands on her hips and waited.

Eddie grabbed Howie's elbow and pulled him away. "Don't say a word," he warned. "Thanks to Mrs. Rosenbloom's love potion, Bailey Elementary is on the brink of war!"

8

Cupid's Cure

"Here comes Carey," Howie warned Eddie. The two boys had fled the cafeteria and were sneaking to their classroom. They ducked into the gym before Carey spotted them.

"Now do you believe Mrs. Rosenbloom is Cupid?" Eddie asked. "And that she invaded Bailey Elementary armed with love potion cookies?"

Howie didn't want to admit that Eddie was right, but he was still shaking from Liza and Melody's fight. "But where are Cupid's arrows?"

"I figured it out," Eddie said. "Instead of shooting people with arrows, Mrs. Rosenbloom is sticking them with those silly heart buttons. She only gives them to victims who eat one of her special

cookies. All we have to do is stay away from people with those buttons."

"We can't run from everyone with those buttons for the rest of our lives," Howie said.

"Of course not," Eddie told him. "Just until school is over today."

"Then what will we do?" Howie asked. "Carey is hunting you down like a cat hunts mice, and I'm about to lose two friends. And if Mrs. Jeepers gets her fangs into Principal Davis, we'll really be doomed. Can you imagine Dracula for a principal? We have to figure something out soon."

"We'll go to my house after school to work on a cure for Mrs. Rosenbloom's love disease," Eddie decided.

Howie moaned and checked to see if Carey was gone. "What will we do if the cure doesn't work?"

"It has to work," Eddie said slowly. "Our happiness depends on it!"

For the rest of the day, Howie and Eddie avoided anyone wearing heart buttons. It wasn't easy to do. It seemed like half the school was wearing them.

During social studies, Carey tried to pass Eddie a love note, but Eddie just knocked it on the floor. Liza and Melody snapped at each other during science and Howie thought they were going to start fighting.

As soon as school was dismissed, Howie

and Eddie scooted out the door and raced down Delaware Boulevard toward Eddie's house.

Eddie's grandmother was in the kitchen. She was famous for her creative casseroles, and she liked to whip up things using unusual ingredients. She looked at Eddie and Howie when they slammed the back door.

"Grandma!" Eddie panted. "You've got to help us!"

Eddie's grandmother tapped the spoon on the side of the bowl. "What's wrong? Are you in trouble again?"

"Big trouble," Eddie admitted. "But this time it's not my fault."

"That's the truth," Howie added. "It's Liza, and Melody, and Carey, and — "

"Slow down," Eddie's grandmother interrupted and showed the boys a heaping plate of sugar cookies. "Have a snack and then we'll talk about this horrible girl problem."

Eddie's face turned the color of milk and Howie held up his hands. "No way!" Eddie snapped. "We've had enough cookies to last a lifetime."

"Well, I'm glad to hear that." Eddie's grandmother laughed. "I guess what they say is true."

"What's true?" Howie asked.

"That rhyme about girls and boys," Eddie's grandmother said matter-of-factly. "Sugar and spice and everything nice — "

"That's it!" Eddie yelped before his grandmother could finish. "I've got the answer."

9

Pucker Power

"Can Howie and I use the kitchen to make something?" Eddie asked his grandmother.

"You're not going to make a bomb or poison, are you?" his grandmother asked.

"No." Eddie shook his head. "Just some cookie dough."

"All right," she said. "But don't make a mess."

Eddie's grandmother wiped her hands on a kitchen towel and went into the laundry room. Before long, the boys heard her humming as she ironed clothes.

"What does sugar and spice have to do with a cure for Mrs. Rosenbloom's love potion?" Howie asked.

"Grandma says that rhyme all the time. It's: *Sugar and spice and everything nice, that's what little girls are made of. Snips and snails and puppy dog tails, that's what little boys are made of."*

"So?" Howie said, scratching his head.

"So, what's the opposite of sweet sugar?" Eddie asked.

Howie looked at Eddie and thought. "Sour puppy dog tails," he said finally.

"Exactly," Eddie said, slapping Howie on the back. "That's the cure."

"Puppy dog tails?" Howie yelled. "I'm not making anything with dog tails in it."

Eddie shook his head. "We don't need dogs. We're going to make something so sour that love will be the last thing anyone thinks about when they eat it." Eddie pulled jars out of the refrigerator and cabinets along with a big bowl and spoon.

"If it tastes that bad, no one is going to eat it," Howie said.

"You just help me make it," Eddie explained. "I'll take care of getting them to eat it."

Howie shrugged his shoulders and reached for a bottle. It was vinegar. He poured half the bottle into Eddie's big bowl. "Vinegar is disgusting. I tasted it one time," Howie said.

"That's the spirit. That'll give it pucker power," Eddie said. "Let's start mixing." Howie stirred the ingredients while Eddie dumped in one thing after another. He added lemon juice, garlic powder, and black pepper.

"It's too runny," Howie said. "We need something to make it stick together."

Eddie nodded and looked inside the refrigerator. He pulled out the mustard. After emptying half the jar into the bowl, Eddie said, "That looks like cookie dough to me. We can add it to Mrs. Rosenbloom's batter and she will never know the difference."

"No, she'll know. This stuff is bright yellow and her cookies are red. This

would make them turn orange," Howie said.

"I can fix that," Eddie said. He whipped a big container out of the refrigerator and squeezed it. The bowl quickly filled with bright red ketchup. Howie stirred and stirred until the mixture was solid red.

Howie and Eddie looked in the bowl and smiled. "Perfect," they said together.

10

Hand in the Cookie Jar

Before school the next morning, Eddie and Howie met under the big oak tree. "Did you bring it?" Howie asked.

"Yeah," Eddie said, patting his backpack. "I had to tell Grandma it was a science project to get it out of the house."

"It *is* an experiment," Howie said. "I just hope it works." The two boys quietly walked into the building and straight to the lunchroom.

"Mrs. Rosenbloom's in there," Eddie hissed as they peeked into the kitchen. The two boys saw the red-dressed cook sitting at a counter making heart-shaped sandwiches. Behind her was a big bowl of cookie dough.

As the boys were watching, Mrs. Rosenbloom started singing, very loudly and off-key. "I *love* Valentine's Day . . ."

Eddie giggled. "I wish she'd quit that racket. She's hurting my ears."

"My *love* is higher than the highest mountain!" Mrs. Rosenbloom bellowed as she added cheese to the sandwiches.

"She belongs high on a mountain," Eddie said, "like way in the clouds."

"Let's forget the whole thing," Howie whispered. "We'll never be able to sneak past her."

"She's singing so loud, she'll never hear me. Just watch," Eddie said, pulling a big plastic bag from his backpack. Then he dropped to the floor and started crawling, holding the bag with his teeth. He crawled until he was right behind Mrs. Rosenbloom. Very slowly, Eddie stood up and dumped his anti-love potion into the big bowl of cookie dough. Eddie had just started mixing it when he felt something grab his cheek. It was a big hand with bright pink fingernails.

"Happy Valentine's Day, little boy. Looks like you've been caught with your hand in the cookie jar!" Mrs. Rosenbloom said, still holding on to Eddie's cheek.

Eddie's face turned as red as Mrs. Rosenbloom's lipstick. "I . . . I . . . I just wanted to taste one of your famous cookies. Everybody says they're delicious."

Mrs. Rosenbloom smiled and let go of Eddie's cheek. "Why, thanks for the compliment, honey."

"But I understand if you don't have any made yet," Eddie said quickly. "I'll just have to wait."

"Don't be silly." Mrs. Rosenbloom grabbed Eddie's arm and pulled him across the kitchen. "I happen to have one left from yesterday. I only give these to good friends, but you look pretty special to me."

Mrs. Rosenbloom held up a large red cookie. It was covered with globs of red sugar crystals. "Don't be shy," she said. "You can eat it."

Eddie opened his mouth to say, "No, thank you." But he didn't get a chance. As soon as he opened his mouth, Mrs. Rosenbloom stuck the cookie in.

"Yum!" Eddie said, with his mouth full. "This is delicious!" While Eddie was busy chomping on the cookie, Mrs. Rosenbloom quickly put a heart button onto his shirt.

"You're all ready for Valentine's Day," Mrs. Rosenbloom said. "Run along now."

Eddie met Howie back out in the hall. "Did you have to eat a cookie?" Howie squealed.

"I didn't have a choice," Eddie complained. "Besides, I'm too tough for a love potion to work on me."

"I hope you're right," Howie said, "because here comes Carey."

11

Head Over Heels

"Wow!" Eddie whispered. "Look how Carey's hair bounces!"

Howie grinned. "If it bounced any more, we could use her head for a basketball."

"And it's so shiny," Eddie continued as if he hadn't heard a word Howie said. "I just *love* it."

Howie stopped and stared at his best friend. "What did you say?"

"I just noticed how nice Carey looks, that's all," Eddie said.

Eddie smiled at Carey and Carey smiled back. She was looking at Eddie and didn't watch where she was going. *Wham!* Carey walked right into Ben, the meanest, toughest bully in the entire fourth grade.

They both fell, scattering books and homework all over the floor.

"I'd better help. Ben's liable to beat her up." Eddie rushed over to Carey and helped her up. Then he scrambled to pick up her things.

"Sorry," Ben apologized. "I didn't mean to run into you."

"What's got into him?" Eddie asked as Ben walked away. "He's usually so mean."

Carey shrugged her shoulders. Then she batted her eyelashes at Eddie. "'It was because you were protecting me. You probably saved my life."

Eddie stood up straight. "It was nothing. I'd be honored to carry your things to class," he said in his best grown-up voice.

"Pssst! We have a mission to complete," Howie called from across the hall.

"Can't you see I'm busy?" Eddie snapped. "Carey needs my help."

"But what about our plan?"

"What plan?" Carey asked sweetly.

Eddie smiled at her. "Howie and I were doing a little cooking, but I don't want to anymore."

"What about Mrs. Rosenbloom's cookies?" Howie said.

"Mmmm." Carey patted her stomach. "Those are the best cookies I've ever tasted."

"Maybe you should try one," Eddie told Howie. Then Eddie walked Carey into the classroom.

Howie slumped against the wall. "He's head over heels for Carey. Now what am I going to do?"

"It looks like you need some sweetening up," a voice echoed in the hall.

Howie jumped to see Mrs. Rosenbloom staring at him. "I don't need anything," he said.

"Now, sweetie, you're as sour as lemon peels. One of my special cookies will put a smile on your face."

"N-n-no thanks," Howie stammered and backed around a corner. He ran right into Liza and Melody.

"We've been looking all over for you," Melody said. "Have you decided yet?"

"Decided what?" Howie asked.

"Which one of us you like better, silly." Liza giggled.

Howie glared at the girls. "I'm beginning to think I don't like either of you."

Liza sniffed. "How dare you even think that!"

"I'm sorry," Howie said. "I didn't mean it."

"Well," Melody said loudly and crossed her arms. "You're going to have to decide and that's all there is to it." Liza crossed her arms and tapped her foot on the floor. Both girls stared at Howie.

"I . . . I . . ." Howie began.

"Yes?" Melody and Liza leaned close to Howie.

Howie took a deep breath. There was

only one thing to say. "I will make my decision right after lunch."

Both girls walked into the classroom whispering, "I bet he likes me better."

Howie gulped. He knew he wouldn't feel much like eating lunch today. He hoped that Mrs. Rosenbloom hadn't seen Eddie throw the anti-love potion into her cookie batter. It was his only chance. As a matter of fact, it was the only chance for Bailey Elementary.

12

Puppy Dog Tails

By lunchtime, Howie was feeling sick. He walked by himself to the lunchroom. Everyone else was blowing kisses and making goo-goo eyes at each other.

Filing through the lunch line, Howie caught a glimpse of Mrs. Rosenbloom's newest batch of cookies. There was a huge heart-shaped tray piled high with them. But today the cookies weren't bright red, they were sort of brown and splotchy.

"Yes!" Howie said to himself. The anti-love potion was in there, but would it work?

Mrs. Rosenbloom shook her head. "I'm not sure what happened. I followed my usual recipe, but today they look different. And for some reason there's enough

for the entire school. Help yourself."

Kids grabbed handfuls of the cookies and the pile dwindled away. Howie took his tray to a table in the corner of the cafeteria. He picked at his heart-shaped potato cake and looked around the room.

Eddie was giggling with Carey at a table in another corner. Liza and Melody were winking at him. Ben and Issy were staring into each other's eyes. Even Mrs. Jeepers was giving half her sugar cookie to Principal Davis.

Howie held his breath. People were eating the cookies!

"Yuck!" Principal Davis bellowed, spitting cookie everywhere. "This is the worst cookie I've ever tasted! What's in them?"

Puppy dog tails, Howie chuckled to himself.

Mrs. Rosenbloom rushed out of the kitchen as kids all over the cafeteria complained about the cookies. "What's wrong?" she asked.

"These cookies are horrible," Principal Davis told her.

Mrs. Rosenbloom shook her head and rushed back into the kitchen. "I don't understand. I didn't change the recipe one bit."

The next day at lunchtime, Liza and Melody brought their lunch trays over to sit with Howie.

"There's not a trace of yesterday's valentines," Melody said.

"This place looks so ordinary now," Liza said sadly. "I liked all the decorations." The three kids looked around the cafeteria. Not a single red or pink heart remained anywhere.

"I guess Mrs. Rosenbloom took them with her," Melody said. "I heard Principal Davis telling the secretary that she was moving to the mountains. She wanted to be up near the clouds on the mountaintop," he said.

"I guess we're free from Cupid's spells now." Howie sighed.

"Until next Valentine's Day," Liza added.

Eddie brought his tray and sat down beside them. "I fixed Carey." He giggled. "When she wasn't looking, I put pepper in her milk."

"I thought you liked Carey," Howie said.

Eddie rolled his eyes. "Are you crazy? I can't stand her."

Howie looked at Melody and Liza. "Are you guys still mad at each other?" he asked.

"What are you talking about? We never fight," Melody said.

"So we're still friends?" Howie asked hopefully, glad that things were getting back to normal.

"Of course," Melody and Liza said together. "We *love* being your friends."

Gremlins
Don't Chew
Bubble Gum

To the members of Writers Ink in Lexington, Kentucky, with special thanks to Alexis, Jerrie, Joel, Mark, Becky, Janice, Tom, and Wendy for helping us find the gremlins in our writing.
— MTJ and DD

1

Pop!

Snap! Pop! The lights in the third-grade classroom went out. The only light came from the windows along one wall.

"It's a blackout!" shrieked Liza.

Eddie jumped out of his seat, his curly red hair bouncing. "All right, we get to go home! We can't have school in the dark."

Mrs. Jeepers, their teacher, cleared her throat. "Students, I am sure everything will be fine. Principal Davis will make an announcement about this unfortunate electrical failure."

The students waited and waited. Then they waited some more. But the lights stayed off and there was no announcement. Melody and Liza yawned, and Howie tapped his pencil on his desk.

Eddie wiggled and squirmed until he fell out of his seat.

Everybody laughed. Everybody, that is, except Mrs. Jeepers. She touched her green brooch and all the students suddenly got very quiet. Whenever Mrs. Jeepers touched her brooch, they knew they had better shape up . . . or else. Most of the third-graders thought Mrs. Jeepers was a vampire. Even Eddie slid quietly back into his seat.

Carey stuck her hand into the air. "I'd be happy to take a note to the secretary."

"That is an excellent idea," Mrs. Jeepers said as Carey smiled. "But it is Melody's turn to deliver a message."

Mrs. Jeepers quickly jotted a note and handed it to Melody. "Please take this to Miss Kidwell," Mrs. Jeepers said.

"Who?" Melody asked.

"Ms. Moore, the regular secretary, is on her honeymoon," Mrs. Jeepers said. "I met her temporary replacement, Miss

Kidwell, this morning when she brought around the lunch tickets."

Carey stuck her tongue out as Melody walked past her desk and out of the third-grade classroom. Melody looked down the long dark hallway and started to turn around to give the note to Carey, but she didn't want the class to think she was afraid. So she took a deep breath and headed into the shadows. It was so dark she had to feel her way by touching the walls. The only light came from her tiny watch.

She had never noticed before how far the office was from her classroom. The office looked at least one hundred miles away. Every room she passed was dark and inside she could hear teachers reassuring their students.

After slowly walking down the tomb-like hall, Melody finally made it to the office. Principal Davis was staring at the electrical fuse box on the office wall. The tiniest woman Melody had ever seen stood next to him. She was wearing a long lime-green dress that was covered with bright orange flowers. The strange woman's jet-black braids stuck out all over her head and sparkled with streaks of silver.

Melody blinked. When she opened her eyes, the woman was looking at Melody, the hundreds of tiny braids hanging limp at her shoulders. Melody couldn't see a fleck of silver in them.

"Yikes!" Melody said to herself.

"What's that, little lady?" the woman asked.

"Uh, lights!" Melody blurted. "There aren't any lights. My teacher wanted me to give this note to Miss Kidwell."

When the lady nodded, her braids swayed. "That would be me!"

Melody handed the note to Miss Kidwell. On Miss Kidwell's right wrist was a bright silver chain. One lonely charm dangled from the bracelet. It was a lightbulb charm.

Miss Kidwell nodded and chuckled. "Your teacher is right. The lights have gone kaput!"

"They're definitely kaput. What this old building needs is new wiring." Principal Davis grumbled and scratched the shiny top of his bald head. "I wonder if one of these switches will turn the lights back on." Principal Davis reached in the fuse box and punched a button. The radio on the secretary's desk blared to life. Then he punched another button. This time, the electric pencil sharpener started buzzing.

"It must be this one," Principal Davis said as he punched a third button. Suddenly, the bell clanged throughout the halls of Bailey Elementary. Melody clapped her hands over her ears and Miss Kidwell started laughing. Principal Davis quickly punched more buttons, but the bell kept ringing. "I've tried everything I can think of," he yelled over the ringing bell. "This is a very tricky problem."

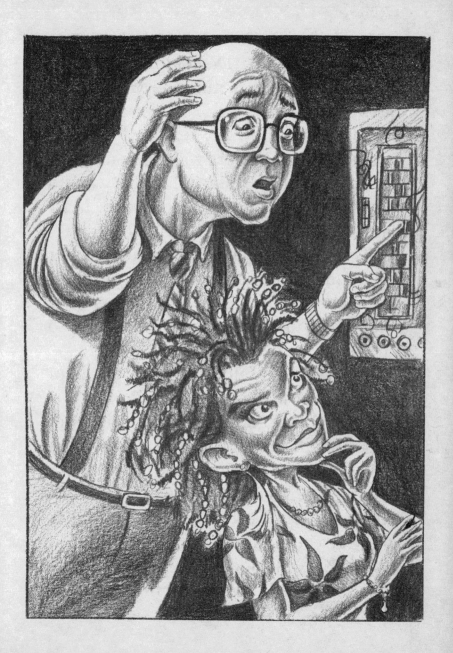

Miss Kidwell winked at Melody. "It's a good trick, all right. You kids can't work with this racket. It must be your lucky day."

"You don't know my teacher," Melody told her. "Mrs. Jeepers will make us work no matter what. Besides, I really wanted to show my science project video, but I can't do that without electricity."

Miss Kidwell placed her hands on her hips and shook her head. "Tsk, tsk, tsk. No need to frown. The problem is only temporary like me! You need lights, so I'll help."

"But when?" Melody asked. "I'm supposed to show my video after lunch."

"Don't worry about the time." Miss Kidwell tapped Melody's watch. "You won't miss that special science class."

Melody smiled. "Thanks. I can show everyone how I used ten different seeds to attract birds to my yard."

Miss Kidwell nodded. "You must be a very smart girl. Now scoot to class."

Melody stopped at the office door and watched Miss Kidwell wave good-bye. Was it her imagination or were there two charms dangling from Miss Kidwell's bracelet now?

2

Time to Play

When Melody got back to the room, the class was lining up for an early recess.

"Perhaps by the time we get back, the lights will be on," Mrs. Jeepers explained and rubbed her forehead, "and the bell will be silent."

"I hope the lights never come back on," Eddie told Melody, Howie, and Liza when they got outside. They were standing under a big oak tree on the playground.

"Miss Kidwell promised the lights would be on soon," Melody told them.

"I hope so," Liza said. "We can't show our science projects in the dark."

Eddie leaned against the oak tree. "I'd probably get a better grade in the dark," he admitted.

"Wait till you see mine. It's incredible,"

Howie told his friends. "It's all about radio waves. My dad helped me with it." Howie's dad was a scientist at FATS, the Federal Aeronautics Technology Station, a nearby research laboratory.

"That's not fair," Eddie complained. "You got special help. I had to make my stupid remote control airplane by myself."

"You're mad because it didn't work," Liza said. "My project's about static electricity. The best part is when your hair stands straight up." She pulled her blonde hair up as high as it would go.

"You look like you stuck your finger in a light socket and got fried," Eddie said.

"That's how the secretary looked," Melody said.

"My aunt says getting married will do that to you," Liza giggled.

Melody shook her head. "I mean the temporary secretary. When I went to the office, her hair was standing straight up and it looked like it had electricity running through it."

Eddie patted Melody on the back. "Maybe she left her electric rollers in too long."

"I'm serious," Melody said. "There's something very strange about her."

"What?" Howie asked.

"I don't know," Melody said. "But I'm going to figure it out."

"Well, while you're figuring, let's play kickball," Eddie suggested. He snatched a ball and raced to the far end of the playground. A few other kids joined them and they quickly chose teams. They played and played until they were out of breath. Then they played some more.

When it was Liza's turn, she rushed toward the big red ball and kicked as hard as she could. Unfortunately, she missed and she fell down in the dirt. "Ow!" Liza said.

Eddie laughed out loud. "Liza can't even kick the ball," he hollered.

Liza's face turned redder than a strawberry. She hopped up, dusting off the seat of her pants. "I can, too," she snapped at Eddie. "But the sun was in my eyes. Besides, I'm thirsty. I need to go inside for a drink."

Eddie laughed even harder. "You just want to go in because you can't play kickball."

"Do not," Liza sputtered.

"I'm thirsty, too," Melody interrupted before Eddie could tease Liza anymore. "But we can't go inside yet. The bell is still ringing." The four kids listened to the shrill ringing coming from Bailey Elementary school.

"You think they'd have it fixed by now," Howie said. He looked at Melody. "What time do you have?"

Melody sat down on the ground and looked at her watch. "Oh, no!" she cried. "It's broken."

"That's weird that your watch and the school clocks would break at the same

time," Liza said, stooping beside Melody.

"That's it!" Melody jumped up. "I just realized what's so strange about Miss Kidwell."

"What?" Liza asked.

"Everything she touches gets messed up," Melody explained.

"Just like Liza." Eddie laughed. "She even messes up kickball."

"No, I mean really messed up," Melody said.

"Like your brain," Eddie said. "Nobod

can touch things and make them mess up."

"Unless she's a gremlin," Howie suggested.

"A what?" Melody, Liza, and Eddie asked together.

"A gremlin," Howie said. "My dad told me about them when we were having trouble with my science project. Gremlins are little creatures that mess up mechanical things."

"I mess up mechanical things all the time at my house," Eddie said. "I guess that makes me a gremlin."

"That makes you a walking disaster," Melody said. "But this thing with Miss Kidwell is serious. First, it was the lights, now our watches. What will be next?"

3

Frozen in Time

Howie looked at his friends. "Melody's right. We might be in the middle of a mechanical emergency. I wonder if the rest of the clocks are working."

"I hope not," Eddie said. "Then we could stay outside all day."

"But I don't want to play anymore," Liza whined.

"You're just mad because you missed the ball," Eddie snapped.

Howie ignored Eddie. "Let's go inside and check the clocks."

"And ruin a perfectly good recess?" Eddie asked.

"We can't stay outside forever," Melody pointed out.

Eddie shrugged. "Why not?"

"Because we have to demonstrate o

science projects," Liza reminded him.

Eddie rolled his eyes. "I don't give a hoot about the science projects."

"Don't come, then," Howie said. "We'll find out the truth about Miss Kidwell without you." Howie walked to the building with Melody and Liza close behind.

"Howie ruins all my fun," Eddie complained and raced after them.

Inside the building, the bell echoed in the empty halls and Liza put her hands over her ears to muffle the sound. "This is giving me a headache," she said.

"School always gives me a headache," Eddie griped.

Howie pointed to a clock hanging on the wall. Everyone looked, but nobody said a word.

"Let's check another one to be sure," Liza suggested.

⸍urned a corner and Melody fast, Liza bumped into her. d at another clock. "They're 10:28," she said over the

266

ringing bell. "That's the exact time I was in the office. I noticed because Miss Kidwell tapped my watch."

"She *is* a gremlin," Liza yelped.

"You can't seriously believe a secretary with crazy hair stopped time!" Eddie said. "The lights went off, remember? These clocks use electricity, too."

"Shhh," Howie warned, his fingers to his lips. "I hear something."

"You'd be in trouble if you didn't," Eddie said. "That bell is loud enough to wake a hibernating bear."

Howie shook his head. "I'm not talking about the bell. There's something else."

"It sounds like popcorn popping, only louder," Melody said.

Liza licked her lips. "I wish it was popcorn. I'm hungry."

"It reminds me of the static on my science project radio," Howie said. "I bet it's coming from the office."

"You're crazy," Eddie said. "You're just hearing static from your brain. There's nothing in the office but a substitute secretary."

Howie gave his friend a dirty look. "If you're not going to help, then go back outside. But the rest of us are going to get to the bottom of this."

"Besides," Melody said, "we still need to find out what time it is."

"All right," Eddie mumbled. "I am getting a little hungry. I'd hate to miss lunch."

"Let's go." Howie led the way down the dark hallway, pausing every once in a while to listen to the strange popping noises.

"The noise is coming from everywhere," Liza whimpered.

Melody shook her head. "It's coming from the intercom."

They turned the last corner and stared into the office. There was Miss Kidwell. Her braids shook and they were glowing silver. She was standing at the intercom system, twirling the dials and chewing bubble gum.

"Look at her hair," Melody squeaked. "I told you she had silver streaks."

Eddie squinted. "You're just seeing things."

"Well, if it isn't the scientist," Miss Kidwell said, facing the kids.

"We need to know if it's lunchtime," Eddie blurted. "I'm hungry."

"All the clocks are frozen in time," Melody interrupted. "We've been outside forever."

"Isn't that good?" Miss Kidwell laughed. "A day in the sunshine."

"That's what I said," Eddie told her. "But these goody-two-shoes want to show their science projects."

"Besides, we're tired," Liza said. "You can only chase a ball so long!"

Miss Kidwell laughed again. "Tired of playing? I've never heard of such a thing. But don't worry, it is time for recess to end." Miss Kidwell's bracelet with her two charms made a tinkling sound as she pointed at Melody's watch. Then Miss

270

Kidwell blew the biggest bubble the kids had ever seen.

"Now, outside before your teacher misses you." Miss Kidwell scooted the kids out into the hall and watched them turn the corner. But the four friends peeked back around the corner and saw Miss Kidwell blow another huge bubble the size of a tennis ball. She climbed up on a step stool and reached her hand out, touching the electrical fuse box. Then she sucked in the bubble with a huge *pop!* Immediately, the lights flickered on and the bell stopped ringing. The kids shivered. For some reason, the sudden silence was worse than the bell. Much worse.

4
Charming

"Did you see her hair?" Melody squealed when they were in the lunchroom. "It was alive!"

Eddie shook his head. "I'm telling you, she was just chewing that big wad of gum too hard."

"It's not right," Liza complained after sipping her chocolate milk. "It's against the rules to chew gum in school."

"At least we know she's not a gremlin," Eddie said.

"What makes you say that?" Melody asked.

"I'm pretty sure that gremlins don't chew bubble gum," Eddie said and took a bite of his cold pizza. Everything was cold because there was no electricity that morning.

"Gum doesn't mean anything, but her charm bracelet does," Melody said.

"What does a bracelet have to do with anything?" Eddie asked.

Melody wiped her mouth with a napkin and spoke slowly. "The first time I saw her, she only had one charm on her bracelet. Now there are three."

"Who cares about jewelry?" Eddie muttered.

"You should care," Melody explained. "Because one of the charms was a light-bulb and another was a clock."

"So?" Eddie said.

Melody rapped her knuckles against Eddie's head. "Hello, anybody in there? Don't you get it?"

Howie, Liza, and Eddie all shook their heads.

Melody rolled her eyes. "You guys would never make it on a game show. I have to tell you everything. Miss Kidwell is a gremlin and every time she messes something up, she gets a new charm."

"Every time I mess something up, I get in trouble." Eddie laughed. "I should have about a million charms by now. I couldn't even carry my bracelet it would be so heavy."

Liza and Howie laughed, but Melody frowned. "You guys aren't taking this seriously. Miss Kidwell is ruining Bailey Elementary."

"Don't get your shorts all ruffled," Eddie said after gulping the last of his milk. "So far we've had a long recess and haven't had to show our science projects. To me, it's been a great day."

"Here comes Mrs. Jeepers," Liza said. "It's time to show our science projects now." Eddie groaned as all the kids lined up behind their teacher.

"I am sorry, students," Mrs. Jeepers said when they were back in their classroom. "Because of the electricity problem, we will only have time for a few science project demonstrations today. We will save the rest for tomorrow."

Howie raised his hand and volunteered. "I'd be happy to go first." Mrs. Jeepers nodded and Howie carried his project to the front of the room.

"My dad explained it to me, but I built this radio all by myself," he said proudly. "Radios work by receiving electromagnetic waves through the air."

Mrs. Jeepers smiled her odd little half-smile, but Eddie raised his hand. "Can't we hear it?" he asked.

"Certainly," Howie said proudly, and with a click he turned a knob. *Squeal! Squeal!*

The entire class covered their ears. "Ouch!" Liza whined. "Turn it off!"

"I don't understand," Howie said. "It worked perfectly last night. It probably just needs tuning." Howie fiddled with the knobs, but the squealing continued. The entire class had their heads on their desks, covering their ears with their arms.

Mrs. Jeepers tapped Howie on the shoulder. "It is a fine project," she said,

"but perhaps you should turn it off."

Howie's shoulders slumped as he turned off the radio and carried it back to his seat. He didn't say a word while Carey and Melody showed their projects.

After school, under the oak tree, Howie kept muttering, "It worked perfectly last night. I just don't understand."

Liza pointed as Miss Kidwell climbed aboard a school bus. "That's strange," Liza said. "She's riding the school bus home."

"I'll tell you what's strange," Melody told her friends. "Remember when we went into the office and Miss Kidwell was playing with the knobs on the intercom?"

"She was trying to figure out how to use it," Howie explained.

"Or she was sabotaging things with knobs," Melody said. "When I looked at her bracelet, there was a new charm on it. And it was a radio!"

5

Dark Ages

"That temporary secretary is causing an electrical emergency," Melody said, leaning against the oak tree.

Eddie laughed. "The only thing temporary around here is your sanity!"

"You have to admit," Liza said, "it's mighty odd the way everything Miss Kidwell touches goes on the blink."

"Like a gremlin," Howie said with a nod.

"Just because your dad mentioned them, you think you're an expert," Eddie blurted. "But what do you really know?"

Howie shrugged. "You have a point. Maybe we are jumping to conclusions."

"But we have to do something," Melody said, "before Miss Kidwell takes Bailey City back to the Dark Ages."

"What would be wrong with that?" Eddie asked, grabbing onto a low branch and climbing into the tree. "If there wasn't any electricity, maybe they'd cancel school forever!"

"And we couldn't have television," Howie reminded him.

"Or CD players," added Liza.

"Or video games," finished Melody.

Eddie slid down the trunk of the tree. "This *is* serious. We have to do something!"

"But first, we need more information," Howie told his friends. "And I know just the place."

"Where?" his three friends asked at once.

"FATS!" Howie told them. "Meet back here in ten minutes with your bikes."

Fifteen minutes later, the kids started the long ride to the Federal Aeronautics Technology Station. FATS was located at the very edge of Bailey City. It took them nearly a half hour just to get there.

They leaned their bikes against the eight-foot-tall wire fence that circled the station.

"I didn't realize it was so far," Liza panted, trying to catch her breath. "It took forever to get here."

"We could've been here in half the time if you had put more power into pedaling," Eddie griped.

"Liza went as fast as she could," Melody interrupted. "And we're here. So stop complaining."

"Fine," Eddie snapped. "But how are we going to get past this fence?"

"No problem." Howie walked up to a small post by the driveway and pushed a big button. Static exploded from a little black speaker perched on top of the post.

"May I help you?" a woman's voice boomed from the box.

"It's Howie Jones. I'm here to see my dad."

The box was quiet for a few seconds before the static continued. "Please follow the drive to the front door."

Slowly the tall gates swung open. As soon as the four friends were inside, the gates shut with a loud clang.

"How can your dad work all locked up like this?" Melody said with a shiver.

"We're locked up every day in school," Eddie mumbled. "And they expect us to work."

"We're not really locked up," Liza said.

Howie ignored Eddie and Liza. "They have to be careful," he told Melody as he led the way toward the sprawling concrete building. "FATS is involved in top-secret experiments."

A pretty woman in a long white lab coat met them at the front door. She glared down her pointy nose at them. "Your father is waiting for you."

Howie rushed his friends down a long hallway to his dad's office. They scooted inside and closed the door. Howie's dad was sitting at a computer, but he stopped typing when the kids came in. He looked just like Howie, only taller, and he wore gold-rimmed glasses that kept sliding down his nose. "What's going on?" he asked.

"We have gremlins," Melody blurted.

Howie's dad smiled. "So, you're having trouble with your science projects, too?"

"Yes," Eddie mumbled. "But that's not why we're here."

"We need information," Howie said before Eddie could say anything else. "You told me about gremlins the other night. We want to know more."

"Gremlins are just a joke." Howie's dad pushed his glasses back on his nose. "People like to kid around when things don't work well."

Melody's eyes got big. "Did you say *kid?*"

"And *well?*" Liza added.

"*Kidwell.*" Howie nodded. "Tell us more, Dad."

Howie's dad smiled again. "Gremlins," he told them, "were first mentioned

during World War I when British planes started having mechanical problems that no one could explain. Small things kept going wrong, almost like someone was playing a joke on the pilots. But it happened so much, there was the fear that the entire Allied Air Force would be grounded."

"What kind of problems did they have?" Eddie asked.

Howie's dad shrugged and pushed his glasses up again. "The lights would go off, alarms went berserk, and the monitors gave wrong information."

"Like shrieking bells?" Melody asked quietly, as if she were afraid to hear the answer, "and clocks telling the wrong time?"

"Why, yes," Howie's dad said. "Those are two of the problems many pilots reported."

Howie nodded. "How did they figure out it was a gremlin?"

"Nobody really knows for sure,"

Howie's dad warned. "But there were consistent reports from pilots about seeing a small creature with wild hair messing with the equipment during flights."

"Did they ever catch her?" Liza asked.

Howie's dad shook his head and smiled. "I suppose that mischievous creature decided to go bother someone else with pranks because nobody ever found her."

Melody let out a little groan. "I think we found her! And she's working at Bailey Elementary!"

6

Attack Plane

The next morning Eddie was still trying to get his science experiment to work. Eddie and Melody were under the oak tree looking at it when Miss Kidwell came up behind them.

"Lovely morning, isn't it?" Miss Kidwell said, chewing a big wad of bubble gum.

Melody nodded, but Eddie frowned. "It might be okay if I could get this remote control plane to work."

"What's wrong with it?" Miss Kidwell asked.

Eddie held up the bright blue plane for her to see. "It's dead," he said.

"I've always been partial to blue planes myself," she said, touching it with her hand. Before she let go, she blew a big pink bubble and popped it. "Well, we'd

better get to school before we're late,"
Miss Kidwell said.

"Don't worry," Melody told Eddie.
"Howie's radio didn't work, either." Eddie
sighed and stuffed the plane into his
backpack.

Inside the classroom Eddie was the first
to demonstrate his project. Slowly, he
carried his plane to the front of the room.

"What a lovely project," Mrs. Jeepers
said and smiled her half-smile at Eddie.

"It doesn't work, though," Eddie mumbled.

"Why don't you try it?" Howie suggested. Mrs. Jeepers nodded. Eddie put the plane on the floor and pulled a knob on his controller.

To Eddie's surprise, the plane flew into the air and zoomed around the room. "It's working!" Eddie screamed, jumping up and down.

The plane made two passes around the room near the ceiling and then zoomed lower. It flew close to Melody's head and zipped right past Howie. Liza screamed when it zipped a circle around her head, and Carey fell off her chair when it aimed right at her.

"Turn it off!" Liza screamed as the plane chased her around the room.

Eddie jiggled the dials on his controller back and forth, but nothing happened. "I'm trying," he told Liza, "but it won't turn off!"

The plane roared up to the ceiling, did

a flip, and then dive-bombed right toward Mrs. Jeepers. "Oh, no!" Eddie yelled and leaped into the air. He caught the plane right before it landed on Mrs. Jeepers' head.

The whole class sighed and Mrs. Jeepers rubbed her green brooch. "Eddie, I would like you to take a time-out in the hall," she said.

"But, it wasn't my fault . . ." Eddie tried to explain.

Mrs. Jeepers shook her head and pointed to the hallway. Eddie knew there was no use in arguing. He grabbed his plane and headed out the door.

7

Musical Bus

After school Eddie met Melody, Howie, and Liza under the shade of the oak tree. Eddie was still mad about his science project. "It wasn't my fault," Eddie snapped before they could say a word. "It wouldn't even work last night. Then it almost attacks Mrs. Jeepers. I don't understand!"

"I do," Melody said softly.

Eddie glared at Melody. "You don't know anything!"

"I know Miss Kidwell was very interested in your plane this morning," Melody told him.

"She said that she liked blue planes," Liza reminded him. "Then she touched it."

"Just as she blew a huge bubble," Howie added.

Melody snapped her fingers. "I bet she fixes things when she blows a bubble."

"You can't believe she made my plane fly," Eddie said. "After all, you told me gremlins mess things up."

"If they can mess them up, then they can probably fix them, too," Howie reasoned. "Besides, Dad said they like to play tricks."

Melody giggled. "I think your attack plane was a funny trick."

Eddie was ready to make Melody stop laughing, but a loud noise stopped him. At the bus stop, they saw Mrs. Gurney, the bus driver, scratching her head and talking to Principal Davis. "I don't understand. It was running fine this morning." She kicked a tire, while the kids on the bus clapped and hollered.

"Maybe it's out of gas," Principal Davis told her.

Mrs. Gurney glared at Principal Davis.

"I've been driving school buses for twelve years. It's not out of gas. If you don't believe me, try it yourself." Mrs. Gurney tossed the keys to Principal Davis and watched him climb into the driver's seat. When he turned the key, the engine roared to life. But that's not all that happened.

The bus's horn blasted so loud, Liza had to cover her ears. The kids on the bus laughed as the horn honked out the tune of "Rain, Rain, Go Away."

Principal Davis held his hands in the air. "Crazy horn. It must be stuck. I guess you'll have to drive it this way."

"Are you nuts?" Mrs. Gurney bellowed. "I can't drive through town with the horn blasting like that!"

"You have to get these kids home. They live too far away to walk," Principal Davis told her. "So you have to drive the bus."

Just then, the bus switched songs, blaring out "The Itsy, Bitsy Spider." The kids on the bus screamed and clapped with the song. Mrs. Gurney put her hand on her forehead. "I have a feeling it will take me a long, long time to get rid of this headache."

As the bus drove down the street, Melody, Liza, Howie, and Eddie heard "Mary Had a Little Lamb" echoing across Bailey City. They heard something else, too. Something that sent chills down their backs.

8

A Pretty Good Trick

The four kids turned to see Miss Kidwell on the school steps. She was singing "Mary Had a Little Lamb." When she saw the kids looking at her, she popped a bubble and laughed. The honking stopped and she waved to them.

Melody gasped. "She made the music stop!"

"If you call that music," Howie said.

"You guys are crazy," Eddie said, rolling his eyes. "I've had some pretty tough bubble gum before, but I've never had any tough enough to make magic."

"Shh," Liza said. "Here she comes."

Miss Kidwell laughed as she walked up to the children. "That bus honking was a pretty good trick, don't you think? I've always liked music."

Liza looked at Miss Kidwell for a minute before she asked, "Why didn't you ride the bus home today?"

"That's right," Melody said. "You rode it yesterday."

Miss Kidwell smiled. "You are such smart children to notice. Today, I'm walking to the public library for some exercise. So I'd better be on my way!" Miss Kidwell waved good-bye and walked away from the kids.

Melody watched until Miss Kidwell went around the corner of the school. Then Melody looked at her friends. "Did you see it?" she asked.

"See what?" Eddie asked.

"Her charm bracelet, of course!" Melody shrieked. "She has five charms now!"

"So?" Liza said. "Maybe she got paid and bought some more."

"But doesn't it seem strange that she bought a radio, a plane, and a bus?" Melody asked.

Howie's face went pale. "Those are the

300

things that went wrong or got fixed."

Melody nodded her head. "Exactly. And if we don't do something soon, there's no telling what might happen next."

Eddie laughed. "You need to learn to relax. Maybe you should try yoga. Miss Kidwell is not a gremlin and nothing really bad has happened."

"What about your plane attacking the class?" Howie asked.

Eddie laughed. "I have to admit that was funny, even if I did get in trouble."

Liza giggled. "Eddie's right. Maybe the bus and electricity were just accidents."

"Don't forget about Howie's radio and Eddie's plane," Melody reminded them. "I just hope the secretary gets back from her honeymoon before Bailey Elementary ends up a disaster area!"

9

Bailey Spies

"I know what to do," Howie said. "Let's go!"

"Wait a minute!" Eddie grabbed Howie's jacket and pulled him back under the shade of the big oak tree. "Go where?"

"To the library," Howie sputtered. "Where else?"

"The library!" Eddie yelled. "I'd rather eat worms than go there. I want to play soccer."

Howie rolled his eyes at Eddie. "The Bailey library has all the answers we need. Besides the books, we can do a little spying on Miss Kidwell."

"Spying!" Liza gasped.

"Now you're talking." Eddie grinned. "Spying is almost as fun as soccer."

Melody ignored Eddie. "What can we find out from watching Miss Kidwell in the library?" she asked.

Howie walked away, but he answered Melody over his shoulder. "I don't know. But we have to do something, and the only thing I can think of is to get some facts."

Howie's friends followed him away from the school, down Forest Lane, and into the quiet shadows of the Bailey City library.

"I want to be the spy!" Eddie said.

"Shhh!" Melody warned. "You know how grumpy Mr. Cooper gets about noise."

Just then, Mr. Cooper walked up to the four Bailey students. His footsteps echoed on the wooden floors. He put his hands on his hips and squinted his eyes. "I am in no mood for mischief," he warned. "I don't want to hear any complaints about you kids."

"Yes, Mr. Cooper," Howie said politely.

"We won't cause any trouble," Liza said.

"Humph, I hope not," Mr. Cooper muttered before walking away.

The kids weaved up and down aisles of books until they reached the section filled with encyclopedias and dictionaries. Howie looked at his friends. "Spread out and find Miss Kidwell while I look up information about gremlins."

"What do we do if we see her?" Liza asked.

"Try to see what books she's looking at," Howie suggested.

Liza and Melody nodded, but Eddie groaned. "I've never heard of spies reading books before."

Howie shrugged and started searching the shelves. Melody, Liza, and Eddie disappeared down another aisle. They hadn't gone far when they spotted Miss Kidwell. Her black-and-silver braids bounced as she chewed a huge wad of gum. She was concentrating on a big blue book.

"Can you see the title?" Melody whispered.

Liza and Eddie shook their heads. "I'll find out," Eddie whispered and sneaked down the aisle. He crouched low and maneuvered close to Miss Kidwell. Liza covered her eyes and Melody held her breath. But Miss Kidwell was too busy reading to notice Eddie's curly head peering up at her from the other side of the bookshelf. Then his head disappeared and soon Eddie was standing next to Melody and Liza. "I told you I'd make a good spy," he said with a grin.

"What was her book about?" Melody asked.

Eddie shrugged. "She's reading about the Federal Aeronautics Technology Station."

"That's odd," Liza said. "Why would she want to know about FATS?"

"I don't know," Melody said slowly.

"But I think we should tell Howie."

Howie was sitting at a long table with a huge book in front of him. "Here's the truth about gremlins!" Howie said as his friends walked up.

"Why don't you check that book out?" Eddie suggested. "That way we could still play soccer for a while."

"I tried to," Howie told him. "But all the library computers crashed. No one can check out a book anywhere in Bailey City."

Just then, laughter sounded from behind them. "Now why would you need a book about gremlins?" Miss Kidwell asked.

Slowly, the kids turned to see Miss Kidwell. The first thing they noticed was the shiny new charm dangling from her bracelet. And it was a computer!

10

Invaded

The next morning, Howie kicked a clod of mud and threw his backpack on the ground near the trunk of the giant oak tree.

"What's wrong with you?" Melody asked. "You look like you haven't slept all night."

"I haven't," Howie snapped. "FATS was invaded!"

"When? How? Why?" his friends asked.

"It happened just after dark," Howie explained. "But nobody can figure out how or why!"

"Then how do you know it was invaded?" Eddie asked.

"Because every computer, every light, and every piece of machinery just quit working . . . all at the same time!" Howie told them.

"Wait a minute," Melody gasped. "I know what happened."

Howie scowled. "Famous scientists can't explain it. How can you?"

"Easy," Melody told him. "We weren't the only ones at the library, remember. We forgot to tell you what we found out about Miss Kidwell."

"Tell me now," Howie said seriously. "The safety of FATS and Bailey City may depend on what you know."

"Let me tell," Eddie said. "After all, I was the one who found it out."

"What was it?" Howie asked.

Eddie stood tall. "I had to use my best spy moves," he said. "I sneaked around the shelves and looked straight at Miss Kidwell's book."

"Tell me!" Howie shouted.

Eddie crossed his arms and said, "Her book was *Federal Aeronautics Technology Station: A Public Guide.*"

"That does it!" Howie yelled. "First, it was Bailey Elementary. And then the library. Now, it's FATS. The next thing you know, the White House will be shut down all because of a tricky gremlin."

"But what can we do about it?" Liza asked.

"There's only one thing to do," Howie said with a shaky voice. "And I think I know just what it is."

"What?" Eddie asked.

"If we can find the right good luck charm, we can get rid of Miss Kidwell," Howie told them.

Melody nodded. "All we need is something lucky to help us get rid of our bad luck."

"What's the luckiest thing you own?" Howie asked.

"My soccer underwear!" Eddie shouted. "I haven't washed them all season and we haven't lost a game yet."

"That's because you stink the other teams clear to Sheldon City." Melody laughed.

"I have a horseshoe that my dad told me was lucky," Liza said.

"What about the number seven?" Melody said. "That one is supposed to be lucky."

Howie nodded and checked his glow-in-the-dark watch. "Good idea, and I have a wishbone that I've been saving. It's bound to be good luck. If we hurry, we can get the charms and be back before school starts."

"And if we're really *lucky*," Eddie said, "one of these will get rid of Miss Kidwell and our gremlin troubles will be over."

11

Good Luck

In ten minutes the kids were back under the oak tree with their good luck charms stashed in their backpacks. "How are we going to get all this stuff to Miss Kidwell?" Liza asked.

"No problem," Eddie said. "I'll fly my plane around the room and Mrs. Jeepers will send me to the office. I can dump everything on Miss Kidwell's desk."

Howie shook his head. "We have to sneak in without her knowing it."

"We can each ask to go to the bathroom," Melody suggested.

"Good idea," Howie said. "We'll have to go one at a time. And be careful! There's no telling what Miss Kidwell might do if she finds out our plan."

Melody, Eddie, and Liza grabbed their

backpacks and followed Howie into the school.

At eight-thirty, Howie asked to go to the bathroom. When he got to the office, Miss Kidwell had her back to him. While she was busy pouring a cup of coffee, Howie dropped his wishbone into her pencil cup.

He winked at his friends when he sat back down at his desk. Fifteen minutes later Melody asked to go to the bathroom. Mrs. Jeepers looked at her strangely, but let her go. As soon as Melody was out in

the hall, she pulled a paper out of her pocket. Inside the paper was a green magnetic seven that she'd grabbed off her refrigerator door.

Melody peeked into the office and saw Miss Kidwell answering the phone. Melody held her breath and slipped the seven onto the inside of the office door. Quickly, she ran back into the room and made a thumbs-up sign to her friends.

Liza took a deep breath and patted her sweater where the horseshoe was hidden. "Mrs. Jeepers, may I be excused?" she asked.

Mrs. Jeepers touched the green brooch at her neck. "The bathroom certainly is a popular place this morning. Do you really need to go?"

Liza felt the horseshoe in her pocket and nodded. "It is an emergency," she said.

"Very well, then," Mrs. Jeepers said before turning to write math problems on the blackboard.

Liza was gone almost ten minutes before returning to the classroom.

"Did you do it?" Eddie whispered.

"Yes," Liza said. "I put the horseshoe in her desk."

Eddie raised his hand. "Mrs. Jeepers, may I go to the bathroom?" he asked.

Mrs. Jeepers put her hands on her hips and flashed her green eyes at Eddie. "This bathroom epidemic has to stop. Try to wait until after computer time."

"Yes, ma'am," Eddie said politely. Then under his breath he whispered to Howie, "I didn't want to give away my lucky underwear anyway."

In a few minutes, the class lined up for computers. Working in the school's brand-new computer lab was a treat for the kids. There was a shiny computer for each student. No one gave a thought to gremlins or good luck charms as they worked at their computers.

"All right!" Eddie cheered after a while. "I've almost captured all of Planet Zeon.

If I get three more math problems right, I'll be ruler of the universe!"

But Eddie didn't get the chance. With just one more problem to go, every computer suddenly went black.

"*No!*" Eddie shrieked. "What happened?"

"It must be a bug in the system," Howie explained.

Melody nodded. "A very big bug. And her name is Miss Kidwell."

Liza looked ready to cry. "Our good luck charms didn't work. What are we going to do?"

"This has gone too far," Eddie said, staring at his dark computer screen. "Something has to be done and I know just what it is."

12

In the Clover

"Bring your backpacks outside," Eddie told his friends at recess time.

"What for?" Howie asked.

"I'll explain outside," Eddie said. All four kids carried their backpacks to their meeting place under the oak tree.

"What are we going to do?" Liza asked.

"We're going to good luck Miss Kidwell right out of Bailey City," Eddie told them.

"But we don't have any more good luck charms," Liza whined.

"Yes, we do," Eddie said.

"Where?" his friends asked together.

"You're standing in it," Eddie said. The kids looked at their feet. They were standing in a huge bed of clover.

"Clover!" Melody shouted. "Four-leaf clovers are really lucky."

"Exactly!" Eddie smiled. "I don't know why I didn't think of it before."

"Let's start looking," Howie said, dropping to the ground.

Eddie shook his head. "We don't have time. Just fill your backpacks with as much clover as you can."

"There are bound to be four-leaf clovers in here somewhere," Liza said.

"Hopefully enough to help us save Bailey Elementary," Melody agreed.

Howie started ripping up clovers and stuffing them into his pack. "What are you waiting for?" he shouted. "Let's hurry!"

By the time recess was over, their packs were full of clovers. When the bell rang, instead of going straight to their room, the kids took a detour to the office.

"Now what are we going to do?" Howie asked as they crouched outside the office. They could see Miss Kidwell sitting at the secretary's desk, counting milk money.

"Follow me," Eddie said. He strutted into the office with the backpack securely on his back. His friends came after him.

"We have to sit in the office for a while," Eddie announced to Miss Kidwell. "I guess we've been bad."

Miss Kidwell smiled and chewed her gum. "You don't look bad to me, but sit there." She pointed to some chairs by the door.

The four kids sat stiffly with their packs still on their backs. Melody watched as the seconds ticked by on the office clock.

"We'd better get to our room before Mrs. Jeepers comes looking for us," Liza whispered.

"Be patient," Eddie whispered back. The kids watched the clock and then Miss Kidwell.

"Eddie," Howie said. "Maybe we had better get back . . ."

"Look," Melody hissed. The kids looked at Miss Kidwell. Her braids were hanging limp about her head and she was rubbing her forehead. Finally, she laid her head on the desk.

"Are you all right?" Liza asked Miss Kidwell.

Miss Kidwell shook her head. "No, I have a terrible headache. I think I'd better go home right away." With that, Miss Kidwell rushed out of the office.

Eddie jumped out of his seat and held his backpack over his head. "We did it!" he shouted.

"You can't be sure," Melody warned.

"I'm sure," Eddie said. "I feel lucky."

13

Feeling Lucky

The next day all four kids were feeling lucky when they saw their regular secretary, Ms. Moore, sitting at her desk. Scattered all over the office floor were bubble gum wrappers.

"Welcome back," Liza said politely, giving her some flowers. "We really missed you."

Ms. Moore smiled. "Why, thank you. Although I'm sure Miss Kidwell took very good care of you."

"Don't worry," Eddie said. "We'd rather have *you* any day."

"Where did you go on your honeymoon?" Melody asked.

"We went to England. It was fun. We even got to see the Queen!" Ms. Moore

put her flowers in a vase as Principal Davis walked into the office.

"England?" Principal Davis said. "That's where Miss Kidwell went. She's going there to take flying lessons."

"That figures," Eddie muttered.

"What did you say?" Principal Davis asked.

"Oh, nothing," Eddie said quickly. "I was just wondering what Ms. Moore's married name is."

Ms. Moore smiled. "My new name is Lucky, Mrs. Lucky." The secretary didn't say anything else. She just blew a huge bubble and popped it right in front of the kids.

"Oh, no!" Eddie cried. "Not again!"